POOL

OF

DEATH

The Possumwood Mysteries Book 8

HOLLY DEY

ISBN: 978-1-959008-06-4

Acknowledgements

I couldn't do this without the love and support of my wonderful family. I love you so much!

Chapter 1

PRIMROSE CORVINA 'PC' Donovan scratched Guinevere's neck as the donkey munched her hay. She was the seeing-eye equid to Arthur, who stood to Guinevere's right, his empty left eye socket toward his stablemate. Hazel, the three-legged goat, lay under the barn overhang behind her, chewing her cud.

The retired homicide detective turned to her brother. "Okay, Rocky. I've pre-measured all the feed for you. All you have to do is come out in the morning and dump it in the bins, then fill the manger with hay. It'd be nice if you picked the poop and put it in that pile near the side gate for Justice."

"At least I don't have school tomorrow night, since I'm havin' to get up a half hour early," he grumbled.

PC clenched her jaw, so she didn't snap at him. Rocky was trying to get his life together. He'd been clean since last Christmas. Almost eight months was probably his longest stretch of sobriety since before he started drinking, and she understood how fragile it still was.

She ran her hand along Gwen's back as she moved away. "Now, make sure you stay on Arthur's right side so he can see you. If you sneak up on his left and startle him, Gwennie will come after you and bite the fire out of you."

"I kinda wish Mama'd get rid of 'em. She's doin' good after her surgery. She's walkin' better than before she got her new hip. But if she's out here and these donkeys start actin' up and she gets knocked down…" He shrugged.

The detective started toward the gate between the livestock pen and the back yard. "I know. That's why I'm here doing it."

"Yeah, but you're hankerin' to get back to Houston, aren't you? Between work and night school, I don't have time to do all this on the regular."

"I know." PC moved through the gate and waited for Rocky to close it behind him. "Since I'm a retired cop, I'm pretty sure I'll get dismissed from jury duty. But just in case I don't make it back tomorrow evening, don't forget to gather the eggs and lock up the chicken coop. Remember, Mama gives the extra eggs to Justice to sell at the farmers' market. Pavarotti and his girls put themselves to bed. You don't have to do anything but lock the door to keep the varmints out."

The detective stepped into the coop and leaned over to pick up one large brown egg and six blue and green eggs from a nest box. She pulled up the tail of her shirt to make a basket for them.

A small beige terrier mix lay panting under the now unspectacular azalea bushes. PC whistled, and he slowly unfolded his legs and stood, then stretched into a perfect downward dog pose.

"Rocky, please let Cordite out to pee in the morning and when you get home, if I'm not here. Mama can probably manage it during the day. He's really good about not going in the house, so don't let him… overflow."

"Alright. I gotta get goin'. I'm already runnin' late."

He led the way to the back door, PC and Cordite trailing behind like ducklings. Rocky pulled open the screen on the back porch to let them in. Marmalade, one of four semi-feral cats who camped out most days on Rose's back porch, gave Cordite the evil eye from his perch on a wicker chair. The dog scampered inside as soon as the door was open wide enough for him to fit through.

Rocky continued through the kitchen, the living room, and out the front. PC gently set the eggs in the sink and rinsed them off.

Rose Donovan came into the kitchen. "Honey, why don't you take a dozen or so of those to your tenant? I'm sure Felicity'd love some fresh eggs. 'Specially the green and blue ones."

"That's a good idea, Mama." PC retrieved a cardboard egg carton from the pantry. "Is Terry here yet?" she asked, packing up the eggs.

"No. He'll be along soon, though. I'm not a toddler, honey. I don't need constant supervision."

"I know, Mama."

The detective was glad Terry lived just two doors down. It had taken her some time to accept the fact that her mother had a boyfriend after the murder of PC's father nearly forty years ago.

Elwood Wilson—Woody, as she called him—her long-ago high school sweetheart, was now the chief of the Possumwood Police. He'd given her a copy of Trey Donovan's case file when she'd come back to town and PC studied that book most nights before she went to bed.

The case that meant the most to her was one of the few she hadn't been able to solve.

The detective fed Cordite and gave him a scratch behind one ear. "You take care of Mama while I'm gone, okay?"

His shaggy tail traced a few half-circles in the air.

PC collected the eggs and her overnight bag, then kissed Rose on the cheek. "Call Daisy if you need anything. I seriously doubt I'll be selected—the defense attorney will take one look at my former occupation and won't be able to strike me fast enough."

"Did you forget your sister's movin' Zachary into his dorm tomorrow? Football practice is already startin'."

"I *did* forget. I'll probably be back before she is. Bye, Mama."

The detective got into her car, queued up a podcast, and started on the hour's drive into Houston.

It felt weird, knocking on her own front door. But PC didn't want to barge in on Felicity. The graduate student had been renting a room in PC's house over the summer. Technically. Because PC had been staying in Possumwood, Felicity'd had the run of the place. As the detective had to be at the Harris County courthouse no later than 7:00 AM, she opted to spend the night in town.

The door swung open. "Ms. Donovan! It's nice to see you."

PC proffered the eggs. "Mama sent these along."

"Oh, wow! Thank her for me."

While Felicity put the eggs away, PC stepped into the living room. A woman dressed in a patent leather corset sat on the loveseat. Low-rise patent leather pants topped stiletto knee-high black boots.

"Hey, Robin."

"PC! It's so good to see you." The leather-clad woman stood up.

"Good to see you, too. How are things?"

"Groovy. I just finished up with my last client for the day and thought I'd come say hello. Have you had dinner yet? We could go to Spinoza's, if you're hungry."

PC glanced at her FlitBit. "Sure. That'd be great. Let me drop my stuff in the bedroom."

"No hurry. I need to change."

Ten minutes later, Robin returned from next door, wearing a flowing cotton print summer dress.

Probably a whole lot cooler than all that leather.

The detective didn't really understand what drove people to hire a professional dominatrix, but it worked out pretty well for her. She had more clients than she knew what to do with.

Robin shook her keys. "I'm driving."

They piled into her fresh-off-the-showroom-floor Porsche Cayenne. PC expected a throaty roar as the dominatrix pulled out of the driveway, but was surprised by the utter silence.

Felicity leaned in from the back seat. "I convinced Aunt Robin to go for the hybrid model. What do you think?"

"Really fancy."

Robin chuckled. "It's still a beast, though."

In about five minutes, they pulled into the parking lot, where the half-lit sign read *Spinoza in the Heights*. They were arriving at the trailing edge of the dinner bubble, and a few patrons trickled out of the restaurant as Robin searched for a parking spot.

Bingo!

An enormous SUV was halfway out of a slot. She whipped in the instant he was clear, probably disappointing a driver who had just pulled in off the street.

It wouldn't be dark for another forty-five minutes or so, and the soggy, oppressive heat radiated up from the asphalt parking lot with a vengeance. It didn't take more than three steps before beads of sweat welled up on PC's skin.

They hurried inside before they stuck to the heat-softened surface. Heel marks from a variety of shoes already marred the speckled black plane.

"Table for three, Susan." Robin smiled at the hostess.

Susan ushered them to one of the few tables with a view. Faux-finish stucco covered the walls, and trompe l'oeil lemon trees framed the window.

A server swept in with a basket of bread and took their drink orders. PC picked up the menu. *What am I in the mood for? Pizza or pasta?*

Her phone vibrated in her pocket. She discreetly checked it under the table, just in case it was Rose. It was an email notification from her friend, Jack Sylmar, who worked at NASA.

The subject read, "Video Clip"

PC's heart skipped a beat. Her focus narrowed to the unopened email on her phone. She tapped the screen.

"Hey, PC. Sorry it's taken so long to get back to you. Finally had a chance to get this cleaned up. I think I've found something."

Chapter 2

PC BREATHED IN deeply, then held it in. She desperately wanted to read Jack's email, but even if it wasn't rude to ignore her dinner companions, there would be nothing she could do about it, at least until after the meal, but more likely, until she got back to Possumwood.

She exhaled loudly.

"You okay?" Robin peered over her menu at PC.

"Fine. I'm just tired. It's been a long day."

Robin nodded.

PC scanned the extensive pasta section. As soon as she set down her menu and raised her water glass to her lips, the server, a youngish woman with pink and purple hair, appeared at the table.

"You ladies ready to order?" she asked, blessing them with a benevolent smile.

Robin gestured toward her niece. "We'll split the Spinoza Special deep-dish pizza."

"I'll have the fettuccine prima vera, bleu cheese on the side for the salad." The detective handed over her menu.

PC took a piece of focaccia. "How's your fellowship been, Felicity?"

"Great. Instead of downtown, I've been at The Ion working with tech startups. The ideas these people come up with… sometimes it's hard to tell if they're visionary or looney."

Robin and PC chuckled.

"But there is one AI project, and I can't go into detail, but it's a crime prediction system. It analyzes crime incident data and makes predictions on where incidents are likely to occur. It can even predict how likely a criminal is to re-offend."

PC waved a roll. "You don't need a computer for that, most of the time."

"The initial results are very promising. I think preventing murders might be better than solving them." Her eyes widened, as if she'd just realized she might have insulted her landlord.

The detective chuckled. "I agree with you a hundred percent. I wish there wasn't a need for homicide detectives. Are you interested in criminology?"

Robin set her glass on the table. "How many episodes of *48 Hours* did we watch last night? I always said you should have applied to the FBI."

Felicity tilted her head. "I took a forensics class as an elective. I liked it. Really interesting."

"Lot of departments are hiring crime analysts." PC wiped butter from her lips.

"I'll keep that in mind." Felicity toyed with a crispy bread stick. "I didn't get into student housing."

"So you're hoping to extend the lease?" PC bit into the bread.

"Yes, if that works for you. It's such a great location."

"Well." PC took a drink. The extension request was not entirely a surprise. "I don't see why not. I think I may be in Possumwood for a little while longer."

Felicity smiled. "Fantastic! I have to tell you, this neighborhood? I kinda love it."

PC pulled out her phone. Jack's email was still there, waiting to be read. She bit her lip and composed a message. "I'll just send myself an email so I don't forget to get the paperwork done."

Robin straightened her napkin. "Are you going to be on that Jackson case tomorrow?"

"I have no idea what that is, but I'll most likely get dismissed. No defense attorney is going to want a homicide cop on the jury."

"What? I can't believe you haven't heard about that. Albert Jackson? The conspiracy guy?" Robin leaned forward.

"What of him?"

The dominatrix raised her eyebrows, as if she couldn't believe PC wasn't up on all the dish. "He's on trial for killing his business partner, but his followers think he's being set up to get him off the airwaves."

Felicity broke in. "Does a podcast count as 'airwaves,' Aunt Robin?"

"Well, he's already been kicked off the big socials. I don't know what else he's got, other than recording himself and putting it on his website."

"I confess I haven't been keeping up much with current events since I've been in Possumwood. Too many local goings-on to keep track of."

"I still can't believe you're going to jury duty tomorrow and don't know about this, though. Stay safe—I've heard the Jackson mob may be planning something at the courthouse." Robin picked up her glass of tea.

PC fought the urge to sigh. "I'm sure everything'll be fine. Most of the time, those guys are all mouth."

Robin frowned. "I'm not so sure about that with these particular guys. Just be careful."

The detective plucked a breadstick from the basket. "Security's pretty tight around the courthouse."

"Even if you don't get on the Jackson case, you might get to meet Mack LeBlack." The dominatrix straightened her napkin.

"Isn't he on talk radio? What'll he be doing there? Running a show, hoping to see a mob overrun the courthouse?" PC asked.

Felicity rolled her eyes. "He's been all over the socials for weeks now, complaining about having to go to jury duty. I'd never heard of him until people started roasting him for getting ratioed on Twitter."

"If you say so." PC reached for her tea.

Robin shrugged. "Don't ask me."

"Ratioed means you get many more negative responses than positive."

The server brought their food, and the conversation stilled.

Once they arrived back at Robin's driveway, PC was eager to read the email from Jack. *What had he found?*

She turned down Robin's offer of a glass of wine, claiming exhaustion. Felicity accepted and followed her aunt into the house.

PC walked across the lawn to her own abode. She put her key in the door and pushed it open. Home, sweet home. But it felt different. Someone else was in her space. Someone she didn't really know. Felicity kept the place spotless. There was nothing concrete the detective could point to, just an off feeling. She dispensed herself a glass of chilled water from the refrigerator door before retreating to her bedroom.

She sat on the bed and opened the email that had been calling to her all night, skipping the preview she'd already read and getting to the meat of it.

"Couldn't clean up the little bit of visible face enough to identify, but clear it's a white male, approximately 6'2". Belt buckle is distinctive. Pixilated because original film was so lo-res. Maybe a rodeo guy? There was a rectangular black and white container on the counter. The killer must have taken it with him, because it wasn't there when he left. Hope this helps."

The detective studied the attached blowup of the belt buckle. Definitely the kind of oversized ones that contestants won at rodeos. In Possumwood, that didn't narrow it down much, though. It might look better on a computer screen instead of on her phone. She'd have to wait until she got back to her mother's house to find out.

She remembered that black and white container. It was probably a little bigger than a box of dried pasta. Mosaic tiles created an abstract pattern, and PC remembered when Trey had brought it home from a business trip.

A two-inch slot in the top allowed for the money to be dropped in. Trey Donovan always collected money for the children's cancer hospital. PC had an uncle she'd never met because he died of leukemia when he was nine.

Somebody had not only killed her father, but stolen money from kids with cancer.

People.

Another email popped into her inbox. It was from one of her former co-workers, Phyllis 'Sulphur' Ackroyd. Two other detectives, Don Hebert and Leslie Flynn, had visited a death scene at a drug house. They'd both touched a table where the dealer had been cutting carfentanil into heroin. Now they were in the hospital. Multiple doses of Narcan had reversed the opiate and they would be fine, just being kept overnight for observation. Sulphur gave the hospital and room numbers, in case PC had time to stop by tomorrow.

Carfentanil was nasty stuff. She remembered her drug recognition trainer saying the Parks Service used it to knock down moose for biological surveys and tagging. Only takes a few milligrams to put a fifteen-hundred-pound animal out. Really nasty stuff.

The detective hugged herself. She'd had dinner with her three friends only last month. Sadly, accidental drugs were part of the job. She'd once witnessed an officer being attacked by a gang member who threw white powder in his face. Turned out to have been a mix of methamphetamine and synthetic cathinones, commonly called bath salts. Poor guy had hallucinated about talking cupcakes and bugs crawling on him for hours.

She felt bad for Narcotics. New designer drugs and lethal combinations of existing substances popped up faster than blisters on a hike in new boots. Drug dealers continued to try to hook customers by adding stronger substances to the base drug and increase profits by cutting in cheap filler. Corn starch. Baby laxative. Rat poison. What were their customers going to do? Call the cops?

I'll probably be dismissed from the jury pool and get to the hospital before visiting hours even start in the morning.

She decided to wash away her disappointment with a hot shower in her own bathroom. PC fetched a towel and a washcloth from the linen closet in the hall while the water in the shower got hot. Once she stepped inside, she felt she was going to melt into a puddle. The detective had forgotten how good the pulsating hot water from the massage setting felt on her back, battering away the tension in her shoulders.

She sat on the bed, automatically leaning over to retrieve her father's case file from underneath. But she hadn't brought it with her. Going through that binder had been her nightly ritual since she'd gone back to Possumwood in January. She put in earbuds and listened to an art podcast instead, her eyelids too heavy to stay open, and the speaker's voice floating in the darkness. Words became meaningless noise as her brain clicked over into maintenance mode for the night.

It started like it always did. PC was in the grocery store, in the produce section. She knew better than to look at the people surrounding her, but she did it anyway. A woman with a little girl. They'd both been shot by someone they should have been able to trust the most, the man who was husband to one and father to the other. The little girl was carrying a plastic horse model. PC had hated that case. So senseless. Once the police tracked him down, he chose to eat a bullet rather than go to jail. Was it justice, or a shortcut?

The man restocking the cabbages was one of her first cases. Bar fight.

The sooner she got to checkout, the sooner this nightmare would be over. She put a couple of peaches in her basket, then turned left and went down the canned vegetables aisle. A lady getting a jar of pickles moved with jerky motions, her arms and legs having too many joints. She'd fallen off a balcony. With a little help from a friend. PC made a U-turn. She didn't want to see the woman's face.

Sleigh bells jingled.

That was new. But the sound wasn't. How many times had she heard those bells on the door of the ShopStop? She moved over an aisle and hurried to the front of the store. But now it wasn't the grocery store.

It was the ShopStop.

The clerk stood alone in the mostly dark store, a blinking fluorescent bulb alternately spotlighting him and casting him into shadow. He was a kid. The sixteen-year-old that was at the store last month when the place got robbed and she and Woody almost got killed.

Footsteps echoed behind her. She turned around but saw nothing but shelves in the gloom.

Badum. Badum. Badum.

PC's heart pounded in her throat. Something bad was going to happen. She knew it, could feel it barreling down at her like an eighteen-wheeler with no brakes.

The clerk.

The detective couldn't just leave him. She had to get him out.

Footfalls again. PC tried to turn, but her feet were stuck to the floor. Not even her head would move. He didn't seem to see

14

her as he passed, the man from the video with the hoodie and the pixilated belt buckle.

Can I pull his hood off?

Her arms would not move.

The light flickered back on. But no boy cashier stood there.

It was Trey Donovan.

"Run, Daddy! Run!" PC tried with everything she had to scream. Nothing came out of her mouth but a few impotent squeaks.

Air flooded her lungs and her eyes flew open. It took her a moment to figure out where she was, and even longer to stop shaking.

She glanced at her FlitBit. 4:37.

Well, I was going to get up early, anyway.

PC arrived at the designated parking area at 6:42. Plenty of spaces. Red and clear plastic shards littered the entrance, apparently from a smashed taillight. A chrome bumper from an older car had been pushed to the side so traffic could get into the garage.

The courthouse was only a few city blocks down the street, so she walked instead of waiting for the shuttle. She passed through the short security line after they inspected her small bag. She followed the signs to the jury pool chamber.

There, an officer traded her summons for paperwork to fill out. A lobby area with some seating was sandwiched between the jury chamber and the tunnel that led to the other court buildings, and, eventually, the parking lot. This lobby had a coffee bar and several vending machines.

There was no place to sit down and write, so PC went into the chamber to complete her paperwork. Once she was done, she looked around the room. It was about two-thirds filled with people. *Is this a good turnout?*

An elderly woman with a gaudy pink crocheted shawl made her think of Rose.

A clump of people surrounded the coffee maker, and another handful lined up at the vending machines for snacks. One man attracted a double handful of people on his own. He wore a wrinkled navy sport coat, sleeves pushed up to his elbows, over a black tee-shirt and black Dockers.

"You know who they should draft for jury duty? Retired people, that's who. Someone has to fill in for me on air today so I can be here. It's a waste of my time! And yours. How much productivity do we lose every day in America to things like jury duty?"

The small group clapped softly.

Must be Mack LeBlack. Does he really believe that, or is it just for ratings?

Another man, arms crossed, snorted with derision. "What is wrong with you?"

LeBlack was taken aback. "Excuse you?" Then a greasy smile slicked his lips.

"You heard me. You don't care about anything but stirring up trouble. Everything's just about ratings, isn't it? You don't have a sincere bone in your entire body."

The talk show host chuckled and spread his hands. "Where are the microphones? The TV cameras?" The sycophants behind him also chuckled.

PC swallowed. There were only about a dozen people sur-rounding LeBlack, but it didn't take a big mob to do damage.

The detective strode over to the angry man and clasped one of his hands in both of hers. "Frank! I can't believe it! How weird is this? Meeting you at jury duty?"

His eyelids fluttered like a June bug under a porch light. "What…?" He took a step back. "Lady, I don't know you, and my name's not Frank."

PC pretended to study his face for a few moments. "Maybe you're right. Sorry about that."

She headed in the direction of the coffee bar, the argument short-circuited. Not Frank stalked into the jury chamber. The de-tective was stirring the powdered coffee creamer into her styro cup when she heard a squeal. Her head was not the only one that whipped around toward the sound.

A man in a red aloha shirt trotted up the hallway, waving a pen. "Mr. LeBlack! Can I get your autograph? You can make it out to Dallas. Dallas Papa—"

LeBlack raised his hands as if to ward off an attack. "No au-tographs today, sorry." Then he turned and escaped into the jury chamber.

Dallas' jaw dropped, then snapped shut. His cheeks flushed crimson as he jammed the pen into his pocket and muttered under his breath.

The sound of boots pounding down the corridor caught PC's attention. Four officers in full tactical gear surrounded the officer at the door.

After a terse conversation, the court officer raised her voice. "Ladies and gentlemen of the jury pool, please proceed into the chamber. There are some armed protesters outside, and we're locking down the building as a safety precaution."

Chapter 3

THE CROWD IN the lobby murmured as the officers directed them into the jury chamber. They were scared, and that made PC nervous. A group of scared people was probably the most dangerous thing on the planet. She sat in one of the front row seats, toward the middle of the room. The detective wasn't sure how many chairs there were, but she guessed at least a hundred, and they were divided into two sections by a center aisleway. At the front of the room was an elevated desk with a whiteboard behind it. A woman in a khaki uniform sat behind the desk, a computer screen and stacks of jury summonses before her.

"Get out of the way!" LeBlack shoved past a trembling chihuahua of a man who hesitated in the doorway. The man stumbled into the woman in front of him.

She whirled around. "What is *wrong* with you?" But her ire was directed at LeBlack, not the unfortunate wretch.

PC cringed as she watched LeBlack's eyes start at the lady's black Victorian boots, travel upward, pausing at her black and purple corseted waist, then stop at her ample, uplifted chest, demurely covered by a cropped black cardigan. He snickered. "Why don't you sit down, freak show?"

She shook her head and a long mane of multicolored hair—lavender, and at least two shades each of blue and green—cascaded in beachy waves almost to her waist. PC breathed in sharply as she saw the woman reach for LeBlack. She half-rose in her chair.

Instead of striking him, the woman snatched his right wrist and deftly flipped his hand palm-side up. Her back was to PC, and the detective heard her gasp before dropping his hand and taking a step backward.

"What's wrong with *you*?" LeBlack growled.

"With me? Nothing. You're the one with the problem. Your life line. It's... how old are you?"

"Excuse me?"

The woman shook her head. "Your life line doesn't look like it goes much past fifty."

LeBlack's face suddenly looked feral. "I don't know what you're trying to pull here, weirdo, but it isn't funny. Don't think I don't know who you are. Did somebody put you up to this?"

"Nobody puts me up to anything. I just call 'em as I see 'em."

He took a step toward her. "The station put on a fiftieth birthday bash for me at the Red Chesapeake last month. We raised money for school supplies for homeless children. It was in the paper, on TV. Obviously on the radio. Everybody knows about it."

"I didn't. Couldn't pay me to listen to that garbage you call a show." She turned on her heel and strode to the other side of the room, where there were a few empty chairs.

LeBlack sneered at her retreating figure. As he stood there, an older lady in a hot pink shawl shuffled towards him.

PC's eyes felt magnetized to the awful garment. She wondered if the person who made it was colorblind, because that combination of hues was headache inducing. It was like a train wreck—she didn't want to look, but she couldn't stop herself.

The woman was almost in front of LeBlack when a folded piece of paper fluttered to the ground from the collection of items she held in her hands.

"Young man? Excuse me?" Her voice was nasal and raspy.

The talk show host scowled. "Are you talking to me?"

"Indeed, I am," she croaked, fidgeting with the blue scarf covering her hair. "Would you mind?" The woman gestured to the paper, the lurid pink fringe of her shawl rippling as she moved. The stark whiteness of the gloves she wore only highlighted the vibrancy of the neon that covered her shoulders and upper arms.

With a dramatic sigh, LeBlack leaned over and picked it up. "Here." He shook the paper at her.

"Thank you, son." The woman patted him with her left hand as she took the paper with her right.

"Ouch!" LeBlack jerked his hand away.

"I'm so sorry." The woman raised her hand and rotated her ring topside out, twisting the finger of the glove a little. "One of the stones fell out and the bent setting is forever catching things, so I keep it turned out of the way."

He scowled at her and continued his search for a seat, wounded hand held to his mouth. His step quickened when he saw the man he'd shoved earlier sitting down with a plastic container in his lap.

LeBlack grinned wolfishly at his victim. "Whatcha got there?"

The other man moved the container to the opposite side of his body. A fresh, red and purple bruise, the size of a silver-dollar, puffed up above his right eye.

"You brought enough to share, right?" LeBlack leaned over the man, plucked something out of the plastic box, and popped it into his mouth before he continued down the aisleway.

Was that a brownie?

PC shifted in her chair so she could get a better view of LeBlack as he continued his path of destruction. He rubbed his stomach a few times, but PC couldn't see his face, so she wasn't sure if it was because the brownie was so delicious, or because he had a bellyache.

The court officer pulled the door shut behind him and locked it.

Behind the desk at the front of the room, the female clerk announced over the PA system, "Everyone remain calm. This is just a precaution. We really appreciate you showing up for jury duty, and we'd like you all to go home safely later."

People murmured, and one woman started crying.

PC's phone vibrated. She pulled it out of her bag—Rocky. Hopefully nothing serious. "Hey, Rock."

"PC? I'm… barn… hay to… *static*."

"Rocky, you're breaking up, badly." *Did he hear me?* She hung up. A single, solitary bar graced the signal strength icon. The detective tried a text instead. "Rock, you're breaking up. Can't understand you." She sent the message and waited. Too much concrete for a cell signal, but perhaps a text could get through. Sometimes worked that way. And sometimes one bar was as good as off the grid.

LeBlack's head turned to the far corner of the jury chamber. The woman with mermaid hair had pulled a chair against the wall and was sitting there with an e-reader, discreetly vaping.

A neon pink shawl caught PC's eye like Velcro. The woman wearing it sat in her chair in the middle of the second column of chairs and crocheted, the strand of yarn disappearing into her giant tote bag of a purse. She must have let her hair down—the detective could have sworn it had been up a few minutes ago. Perhaps it was the blue headscarf she'd been wearing then.

The talk show host was intercepted by Dallas Papasomething, the autograph seeker. PC couldn't hear what they were saying. Based on Dallas' body language, the conversation started out tense and got more relaxed as it continued.

Dallas pulled out a small brightly colored package from his pocket. He took something out of it, then offered the package to LeBlack, who also took a piece.

Gum.

Dallas took the foil wrapper from LeBlack and put it in his pocket. Then the radio personality autographed the notebook Dallas had brought with him.

PC checked her phone. Still no reply from Rocky. It seemed to be about hay, so hopefully he could figure it out on his own.

LeBlack turned an empty chair near the mermaid around to face her and sat down. They spoke for a short time. He pulled out his own vape pen and searched his pockets. Irritation on her face, Mermaid reached into her bag, rummaged around, and pulled out a small object, which she handed to LeBlack. He started messing with his e-cigarette.

Vape cartridge. What kind of honey was on his lips to get her to give him one of those after the way he spoke to her earlier?

She watched them for a minute or two, as people shook and tapped their phones all around her. If she had a signal, she'd catch up on her email. Maybe she could get a message to Rocky that way.

If she had a signal.

The PA crackled. "Ladies and gentlemen. You may not be aware that we have Wi-Fi available." She proceeded to write the name of the network, *HarrisCtyCourts*, and the password, *Jury1*, on the whiteboard. "I hope this helps." She sat back down.

PC tried to connect, but so did everyone else, and all she got was an infinite loading circle. *Guess I'll try again later.*

When she looked back at LeBlack and Mermaid, they had been joined by the man who'd gotten into a shouting match with the talk show host earlier. Not Frank, as she knew him. He had a cup of coffee in each hand. LeBlack took one of them and Not Frank pulled up a chair next to Mermaid.

What's going on outside? There was a sometimes uneasy détente between the City of Houston and protesters. Protests rarely turned to riots.

PC sighed and scanned the room. This Albert Jackson case, though. When she'd woken up in the wee hours, she read up on the man. His followers were as good as cult members. No telling what he'd brainwashed them to do. This could get ugly. She really hoped they'd march around, get the whole thing out of their system, and go home.

She checked her phone again. The loading icon still spun in the middle of the screen.

A woman's cry made PC jerk her head around to see what had happened. All eyes were fixed on the events unfolding at the back of the room. Some people rose to get a better view.

Mermaid was standing up and Not Frank was struggling to keep LeBlack from falling out of his chair. The talk show host moaned and gasped a few times.

The officer and the woman behind the desk rushed to his aid. By this time, Not Frank had helped LeBlack to the floor, and he lay terribly, awfully still.

The officer called for medics on his radio, and the woman started CPR.

"They can't get here! The tunnels are locked down." Horror edged the officer's voice as he turned to his colleague.

After stopping to check for breathing and heartbeat several times, the woman performing the CPR sat back on her heels, shaking her head.

Mack LeBlack, it seemed, was dead.

Chapter 4

WHAT JUST HAPPENED? Mack LeBlack dropped dead. Was it natural causes, or had someone given him a helping hand? PC might find some clues, if they'd let her look at the body.

She wormed her way through the crowd and spoke to the officer. "Excuse me. I'm a retired homicide detective. Can I help?"

He cocked his head to one side. "Why would you think he's been murdered, instead of a heart attack or something?"

"He got into verbal altercations with several people here, and he was… a polarizing public figure. Seems like folks either loved him or hated him. I just want to take a look and see if there were any signs it could have been murder. But you're right. It could just as easily have been natural causes."

"That's up to the Medical Examiner to determine, don't you think?"

PC turned toward the man speaking behind her.

"Hi." He extended his hand. "I'm Art Doyle."

The man looked to be at the upper end of middle age, and his nasal voice was like steam being forced through a rusty pipe. PC hesitated for a moment before accepting the handshake from him. His dark hair could use a trim and a shampoo, but he smelled strongly of soap. The hoodie that sagged from his shoulders was zipped about halfway and tightened around his middle.

Art. Doyle. I'm sure I've heard that name before.

"Nice to meet you, Mr. Doyle. You're right. It's the ME's call, but if it was murder, the person who did it is almost certainly in this room. Doesn't hurt to check things out, since we've got nothing better to do, for now."

"Yeah. Yeah. You're right. I'm a huge fan of Investigation Discovery. *Evil Lives Here. Murder Chose Me.* All the shows. I have every book Ann Rule wrote. Maybe I could help?"

A true-crime junkie. Not sure if this is a blessing or a curse.

"We'll see. As he said, it may just be a heart attack."

PC looked to the officer, who shook his head quickly. "I don't have time. Looks like natural causes to me. Do what you want, but don't cause any trouble. Got enough going on now."

Someone had covered the talk show host's face with a jacket. She'd look at that later.

The styro coffee cup lay to LeBlack's right. Only a small amount, maybe a teaspoon or two, was in the container and on the floor, indicating that he'd drunk the entire beverage except for the dregs.

The vape pen was still between the fingers of his left hand. It was dark blue and could be mistaken for a writing pen at first glance.

She squatted next to the corpse and lifted the jacket from LeBlack's face. The first thing she noticed was how sweaty he was. The fabric from the coat had no doubt absorbed most of what was on his face, but beads of it collected around his eyes and his hair had clumped together in wet mats around his face. She reached toward him, then paused.

No gloves.

PC rose and rubbed her hands, looking at the officer. "You wouldn't happen to have any gloves, would you?"

The officer sighed. "You can have *one*. My name's Toby, by the way. Toby Jensen."

"Thanks, Toby." The detective snapped the purple glove onto her right hand and resumed her examination.

First, she opened one of LeBlack's eyes. The pupil was contracted so tightly that it was barely visible. She wasn't expecting to find any petechiae—he hadn't been strangled after all—so she wasn't surprised there were no red flecks in the whites of his eyes.

Even through the thin nitrile glove, LeBlack's skin felt cool to the touch. Odd. He'd only been dead a few minutes, so he should have still been warm.

Had he been ill? Ill enough to drop dead?

The next thing that she noticed was a bluish tinge to his lips. It was true that all corpses took on a blue-grey hue, but pallor mortis typically waited at least fifteen minutes, usually more, to show up. Perhaps he had some kind of respiratory disease or heart condition, but his mouth had looked perfectly normal when he was using it to insult people earlier. He hadn't appeared to have been in frail health then.

PC examined LeBlack's hands. His nails also had a blue tint. She snapped more pictures. Maybe it could be a circulatory disorder, but she'd seen bodies like this before.

Overdoses, especially opiates.

Her knees crackled as she straightened up.

"Well?" Art asked. "What do you think?"

He reminded PC of a small terrier dog. *Yip. Yap. Yap.* Always has to be in the middle of everything. "I don't want to jump to conclusions, but it does look suspicious."

"How so?" Toby asked.

"You see how blue his lips and fingernails are? I think he might have been poisoned."

"What?" Toby's jaw clenched. "In *my* house?"

PC shrugged. "You got any typing paper and either tape or a stapler?"

He tilted his head toward front of the chamber. "Cheryl probably does."

The woman who had been sitting there prior to her fruitless CPR attempt nodded. "Stapler's right on top. Printer's full of paper."

"So, what's our plan?" Art chirped.

Curse. Definitely a curse. "Why don't you go to the front desk and get me several sheets of paper and the stapler? And a pen."

"I'm on it."

"I'll go with you." Cheryl gave the corpse a forlorn glance.

They turned and wove through the small clumps of people who had stuck together in the aftermath of LeBlack's dramatic demise.

PC watched him go for a moment, then covered LeBlack's face with the jacket again. "Toby, I don't suppose you have anything like a ziplock bag, do you?"

"Why?"

"I wanted to collect the coffee cup and the little bit of liquid still in it for evidence."

He sighed and pulled out a second purple glove. "This is my last one."

"Thanks." PC used her phone to take a few pictures before she picked up the cup, righting it so that the remaining liquid ran back inside. Then she tucked it into the glove and tied the end closed. "Not your usual evidence bag, but sometimes you have to improvise."

Toby frowned. He moved closer to the wall, got on his radio, and relayed the sad news about LeBlack to his supervisor.

Art returned with a half-inch stack of printer paper, the stapler, and three pens. "Here you go. Wanted to make sure you had plenty."

"You certainly hit that target." PC took the supplies. With no other place to write, she leaned over an unoccupied chair and used the seat as a desk.

"Whatcha doin'?"

What are you? Three? "Making evidence collection envelopes."

"Oh! I wouldn't have thought of that."

"That's probably because you aren't a homicide cop."

"You got me. I work at the zoo."

Of course you do. "What do you do at the zoo?"

"Ha! You're a poet and didn't know it."

PC made a noncommittal noise.

"Have you been watching the news? We just got a new Asian elephant named Dolly. Rescued from a circus in Vegas. That was a *long* trip. Hey, I could probably give you a behind-the-scenes tour, if you wanted to meet her."

"Maybe I'll take you up on that." PC went back to her pages.

She finished her notes on the location of the vape pen, then folded the paper into an envelope. Once satisfied the documentation was visible, she picked up the e-cig, dropped it in, and stapled the paper closed.

She had the coffee cup that Not Frank had given him.

The vape cartridge he got from Mermaid.

The stolen brownie was in his stomach.

She took a few pictures of the scratch on his wrist from the old woman's ring.

There was only one thing left. Was the gum he'd gotten from Dallas still in his mouth? PC had ceased being squeamish about touching corpses decades ago. But she didn't like cavity searches of any kind and was grateful that the ME usually took care of the more intimate type.

PC kneeled beside the body, moved the jacket, and pulled open LeBlack's mouth.

"Ewww!" Art shouted. "What are you doing? That's so gross."

The detective raised the index finger of her non-gloved hand to her lips. "I thought you really liked true crime."

Art nodded earnestly.

"This is what true crime is like. It's not all pushpins, string, and corkboards. Or mugging for the camera. To get answers, sometimes you have to dig deep." She lifted LeBlack's tongue and checked underneath.

Her new shadow grimaced.

The detective ran a finger down the outside of his bottom left teeth. Nothing. Then she tried the right. And there, tucked securely against his cheek, was a wad of gum. She raised it in triumph.

Is Art going to pass out?

PC dropped the wad into an improvised envelope and re-covered LeBlack.

Leaning over made her back hurt, so she sat on the floor in front of the chair. While everything was fresh in her mind, she made a sketch.

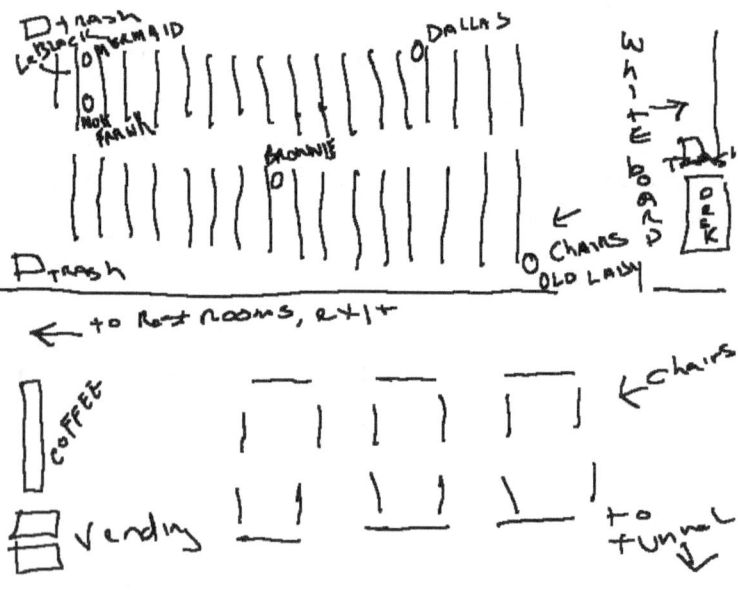

She scanned the room. Mermaid and Not Frank were deep in conversation, in the opposite back corner from the one they'd shared with LeBlack.

Dallas was sitting about a third of the way down, on one of the outside chairs of the second column, tapping his screen and shaking his phone. *Must be on the high speed Wi-Fi we were promised.*

The elderly lady in the hot pink shawl was in the closest seat near the exit—front row, first chair. She held her crochet in her lap, but her hands were still.

The Brownie Man had an aisle seat, about halfway back. He, of course, appeared to have internet, as his head was down and he scrolled on his phone.

They'd need to be interviewed. But would they talk to her? She may as well find out—it wasn't like there was anyone else from Homicide here, and the second that door opened, they risked the killer escaping into the ether.

"Cool map!" Art announced to the entire jury pool.

"Can you keep it down?" *This must be what it's like baking cookies with a toddler.* PC had a surge of respect for Rose, who often baked with not one, but three toddlers way back when. "Don't you have something else to do, Art?"

"No."

Toby returned and started arranging chairs to cordon off LeBlack's body. Given the situation, that was the best that could be done to preserve the crime scene. If it even was a crime scene. It was just as possible that he'd died of natural causes. A blood clot in the lung or heart attack could also cause the blue lips and nails. Best not to have people stomping around the body, either way.

Who to start with?

The Brownie Man seemed to be the least likely suspect. How could he have predicted that LeBlack would shove him and steal his food? Unless he'd encountered the talk show host before and had a similar thing happen.

One way to find out.

PC made her way to where he was sitting, scrolling on his phone. Doyle dogged her steps.

She stopped a few rows behind where Brownie Man sat and whispered over her shoulder. "Would you mind sitting back here and letting me talk to this gentleman alone? He might be more candid, if there isn't a big audience."

"Sure!" The chair scraped across the floor as he moved it to sit down.

Is he trying to alert the Brownie Man, or is he just that incompetent?

The detective approached her quarry. "Hello?"

Brownie Man flinched and jerked his head in her direction.

"Hi. I saw what happened with you and Mr. LeBlack earlier, and I just wanted to talk to you about it. You got a minute?"

His eyes narrowed. "Why? And who are you, anyway? Some tabloid reporter or something?"

"No. Of course not. I'm actually a detective, gathering information for the investigators while we're locked down. I'm Sergeant Donovan, but you can call me PC." She sat in the chair next to him.

"What do you want from me? I didn't know the guy."

PC crossed her ankle over her knee so she could use her leg as a table, then set the thick stack of typing paper down and clicked her pen. "Well, sir, I noticed you had a couple of confrontations with Mr. LeBlack. He shoved you out of the doorway, and then later stole some food from you. Did he give you that bruise?"

He shook his head. "Some piece of work, that guy. I'm Peter Smitherson. Just here for jury duty, like everybody else. Didn't expect Bluto to show up."

The detective tapped her pen on her lip. *He doesn't look old enough to be a Popeye fan.*

"I see. Have you ever encountered Mr. LeBlack before?"

"In real life? No, just on the air. He was a jerk even way back when he first started—what was it? Fifteen years ago? You remember when Hurricane Charlie was in the Gulf and he was constantly on air, sending everybody into a panic? I blame him for a lot of those people dying."

"What do you mean?"

Smitherson exhaled sharply. "Don't you remember? He set off a stampede, so instead of people getting out by zone, the folks who didn't need to evacuate were blocking all the roads so the ones who really needed to get out couldn't. And that bus from the nursing home? The one that got rear-ended and caught on fire, and all those people died?"

PC did remember. Thousands of people were stranded on the freeways in ten-hour traffic jams and ran out of gas, getting stuck with no food or water. Then, of course, the storm turned and hit Louisiana instead. "Yeah. That was over ten years ago, though."

"True, but he hasn't gotten any better. He campaigned for getting the red-light cameras turned off, and now red-light runners are worse than ever. My mother got hit by one of those... idiots. She was in the hospital for a month, and we weren't sure she was going to make it. Still has migraines to this day from her fractured skull." He glowered. "And, two years ago? He almost got the votes turned out to elect B. B. Anthony as mayor. The guy who promised to establish a task force to hunt down the alligators in the storm sewers to improve drainage? That guy was nuts."

"I didn't remember that. Although, I will confess, I don't listen to talk radio."

Smitherson gave her a grim smile. "Probably better for your blood pressure."

"Probably. Did you know he was going to be here for jury duty today?"

"Who didn't know? He's spent the last month or so whining about it on his show. I'm not shedding any tears over him, that's for sure."

Smitherson was a better suspect than she'd thought. Certainly had means. Revenge for his mother's car accident provided motive. Opportunity was a little sketchy. Would he have offered LeBlack a poisoned brownie if the man hadn't stolen it?

PC clicked her pen. "Thanks for your time, Mr. Smitherson."

He nodded. "If somebody did him in, I hope you find them, so they can get a medal for doing a public service."

The detective made a neutral *hmmm* as she stood up. "If I have any more questions, I guess I know where to find you."

Smitherson's eyes turned back to his phone.

PC moved her notes from the conversation to the bottom of the stack.

Okay. Who's next?

Chapter 5

"So, WHAT DO you think? Did he do it?" Doyle padded after PC as she scanned for Dallas, the autograph hound.

She involuntarily cringed at the grating sound of his voice. "I don't have any evidence that he did."

She also didn't have any evidence that LeBlack was murdered. Just a gut feeling. That and blue lips and nails. Cyanosis is much more common with poison than natural causes.

"What about those two he was sitting with? Did one of them slip him something? Maybe... they're working together. Pretty girl distracts him, man slips something in his drink?"

"I suppose that's possible."

Dallas had moved from his seat in the second column of chairs and was now pacing around the front of the room. PC moved to intercept him. Then stopped.

"Would you mind giving me some space, Mr. Doyle? That would really be helpful."

"Sure you don't need me to take notes or anything?"

PC's hackles rose. "No!" she snapped.

Doyle shrunk back, cowed.

"I'm sorry. I didn't mean to bark at you. Can you please just find a seat and let me talk to this gentleman?"

"It's fine. It's fine. We can go over your notes together later, right? I might be able to help you find some inconsistencies in their accounts. That's what they do on the shows."

"We'll see."

Doyle sat down and PC put herself on a collision course with Dallas.

"Hi. Excuse me. Dallas?"

He stopped and turned his sorrowful eyes to the detective. "Yes?"

"Are you okay? It seemed like you were a big fan of Mr. LeBlack."

Dallas shook his head. "I can't believe this has happened. It's such a terrible loss for, not just the city, but the entire region. Cut short in the prime of his life. He would have been such a great rep."

"Rep?"

"How can you not know he was planning on running for the state house of representatives? I'm sure he could have gone straight from there to governor. Such a loss."

"You didn't seem to be too happy with him when he refused to give you an autograph, Mr. Papa—you're not related to the restaurant people, are you?"

"Ha! I wish. No dining empire for me, I'm afraid. It's Papadopoulos."

PC flashed him a bright smile. "Dallas Papadopoulos. You shouldn't have to be famous or well-connected to get an autograph."

"He did come over and talk to me, later."

"I bet it was a happy surprise when you saw him in the lobby."

"Surprise? No, I was ecstatic that I had jury duty the same day as him. He talked about it on his show almost every day. I think he was right when he said that they should either only select retired people for jury duty, or else make it a profession. Something that contributes to the economy."

"That's an interesting take." PC nodded. "Was there anything you disagreed with him about?"

Dallas blinked a few times. "Well. I mean. I didn't agree with him on *everything*. I'm against that zoning ordinance he was trying to get on the ballot. I run my pottery business out of my house. If that thing got passed… I don't know what I'd do. I don't have enough margin to rent retail space." He shrugged. "I did call in to his show about it. Lots of times."

"Really? Were you ever on the air?"

He looked down. "No."

"Did you notice anything strange before he collapsed?"

"No. He was behind me." He tilted his head, eyes suspicious.

"I see. I'm sorry about Mr. LeBlack. Seems like you really looked up to him."

"Thank you."

PC turned and walked back up the aisle. Even though he was a big fan, he stood to lose his business if the new zoning ordinance went through. LeBlack championed the ordinance.

Was that enough of a motive? He might have had means and possibly opportunity.

"Hey!" Doyle yipped at her heels. "What did you find out?"

"Mr. Doyle…"

39

"Call me Art." He nodded. "Call me Art."

"Art. Look. I'm just making some inquiries. I don't know for sure that there was any foul play involved in Mr. LeBlack's untimely death. I'm just trying to have some casual conversations with people who had some disputes with him. That's all. You're making it seem like *Death on the Nile* or something."

One half of Doyle's mouth curled into a sly smile. He winked at her. "Got it. We're keeping it on the QT, so they don't suspect a thing."

PC clenched her jaw. "Yeah. That's exactly it. I need you to lay low while I talk to the next subject."

"You meant 'suspect,' right?"

"No. Please just have a seat and relax."

The detective scanned the room for Not Frank. Mermaid had moved away from him and stood typing on her phone. *Perfect.*

PC strolled to the back corner of the room. Shaking her head, she sat down one chair over from Not Frank. "Such a shame." PC cast her eyes over to LeBlack's body.

"More like Lady Karma." He looked at her and frowned. "You were the one who thought you knew me earlier."

"Yeah. That was me. Sorry."

"That happens to me a lot. Guess I just have a common face. I'm Brady, by the way."

"Nice to meet you, Brady. I'm PC." She glanced at the corpse. "What did you mean about karma? I thought LeBlack was really popular."

"I suppose he is, in certain circles. I couldn't stand him. Such a pompous... Anyway, he'd throw out some insane idea, and his followers would eat it up. Didn't matter how ridiculous."

"Really? Like what?"

"You don't listen to his show?"

PC shook her head.

"Okay. So you know how the county has created these parks that double as flood control? They have ponds that collect water in heavy rain, but most of the time, they're just green space for everyone to enjoy? He suggested that these be permanently flooded and stocked with tilapia. The flood control district could raise money by charging a fee to fish for them."

"That doesn't sound all that crazy."

"Do you have any idea what tilapia do to native aquatic species?"

"Not really. No."

"Tilapia are already a problem invasive exotic. They're prolific breeders and they out-compete native fish."

"But if they're just kept to certain ponds, surely it's not a big problem."

"Do you know how fish seem to magically appear in new ponds? Fish eggs stick to the legs of wading birds, and when the birds fly to a new spot, they take the eggs with them. They could transmit invaders all over the state."

"Oh. You seem to know a lot about this."

"Yes. I'm an environmental biologist. Work for Parks and Wildlife."

"I see."

"And you know what else LeBlack was proposing? He thought it would be a great idea to abolish all regulations on keeping wild animals as pets, and I'm not just talking about raccoons and foxes, but exotics as well—tigers, hyenas, giraffes… anything anybody wanted to have. Do you know how dangerous that could be?"

"Well, I wouldn't want a pack of hyenas living next door."

"But the most unforgivable thing he's done is publishing sea turtle egg recipes and encouraging people to go to the beach and 'forage' for eggs. That alone…" Brady's face darkened, and he clenched his fists.

"But you did talk to him later."

"Yeah. I shouldn't have argued with him. Just makes me look bad, and now he can go on his show and joke about the wacky, tree-hugger biologist. Well, not now. I was hoping I could get him to invite me to speak on his program so I could actually explain why his ideas were… unworkable." He shrugged. "Probably a long shot, and his listeners aren't likely to be reasonable. And that's if I got approval from my boss. It was worth a try, though. That guy needed to be stopped." His eyes wandered over to the row of chairs. "And he has been."

PC sucked her teeth. "Yeah. You're right about that." She leaned over, closer to Brady. "You don't suppose anyone helped him along, do you? Did you see anything, I don't know, suspicious?"

"Not really. Elvira and I were talking to him when he… you know."

"Is that the lady with the colorful hair?"

"Yeah. She's a psychic, tarot card reader, and I'm not sure what else. She has a public access cable show. You ought to talk to her.

See if she can channel the spirits or whatever." His eyebrows flicked up, and he squeezed his lips together.

"Maybe I'll do that." She'd had tips from people calling themselves psychics over the years she was on the job. Most were nonsense. But there was one lady…

PC shifted to look at Elvira and cut her eyes to the ceiling.

Wouldn't that be something, if Elvira could conjure up LeBlack's ghost and ask him what happened?

Chapter 6

PC WAITED PATIENTLY for Elvira to finish her text message. The woman finished typing and tucked a sky-blue lock of hair behind her ear and stared at the screen. Moments later, her shoulders slumped and her head rolled back so her eyes were cast up to the ceiling. She sighed and tapped the screen again. A frown creased her dark red lips, and she muttered to herself, shoving her phone into her bag.

The detective approached.

"Did he send you over here?" Elvira's eyes landed on Brady.

"He did suggest—"

"It's too soon." The psychic shook her head. "You'll have to wait at least three days, maybe a week. They can't communicate with us right away."

PC's jaw slackened, and she tried to disguise it by taking a deep breath. "That's not exactly what I had in mind, but good to know." *I guess.*

"What is it you want, then?"

The detective had to wrench her eyes away from the woman's sparkling septum piercing. "Well, you were speaking with Mr. LeBlack when he… passed. I was just wondering if you could describe what happened? I mean, I was a little surprised to see you hanging out with him after he made fun of your hair earlier."

Elvira's eyes narrowed. "Why is that your business?"

PC glanced around, then stepped closer to the psychic. "I'm a detective. Just trying to collect information about a suspicious death for when the doors open and people scatter."

"Why is it suspicious? Didn't he just have a heart attack?"

The detective gave a half laugh. "Possibly. But we won't know for sure until the medical examiner takes a look. I wanted to check things out, in case it wasn't natural causes."

Elvira twirled a section of blue, green, and purple hair around her finger, seemingly trying to decide what to do. Then she grabbed PC's right hand, palm up.

"I—"

"Hush."

The psychic studied PC's hand, her lips pursing from time to time. At last, she spoke. "Square palm, long fingers. You enjoy intellectual pursuits. Jives with being a detective." Elvira ran her finger along a line that encircled PC's thumb. "There's a star on your life line."

"Is that good?"

"No. But you do have an 'M' here in the center of your palm." She traced intersecting lines that could form the letter, perhaps, if one was looking for it. "That's rare, and very lucky. Maybe enough to cancel out the star. Something very bad happened to you when you were young."

PC shrugged. "That's probably true of a lot of people."

"Not like this. You see how your line of fate intertwines with your life line?" Elvira ran her finger from the center of the heel of PC's hand up to about the base of her thumb. "It separates when it meets the star, then goes all the way to your head line. This is something that shaped your entire life."

The detective pulled her hand away. Lines in a person's hand came from bending fingers, over and over again. They didn't mean anything. "That's an interesting interpretation."

Elvira's lips curled into a demi-smile. "What did you say your name was, Detective?"

"Donovan. But you can call me PC."

The psychic dug in her purse for a moment, then pulled out a silver business card holder with an inlaid enamel fairy. "In case you have any questions about your love life. Or anything else." She handed a card to PC.

ELVIRA RAVENSTONE

†aROT † PALMISTRY † PSYCHIC MEDIUM

Her number, website, and Etsy store were on the back.

PC felt she was getting the brush off, but she wasn't ready to retreat. "So, Elvira. What did he say to you after that little spat this morning?"

The psychic snorted. "He was trying to sweet-talk me into going on his show. I gave him a big fat 'no.' I mean, why would I? If you drew a Venn diagram of my audience and his, you'd have two circles at the opposite ends of the paper."

"Your audience? Is that the cable access show Brady mentioned?"

"Of course. It's not some deep, dark, secret. I want people to watch my show—trying to grow my business, you know?".

PC nodded. "Why do you think he wanted you to come on air with him?"

"I take it you don't listen to his show?"

"No."

"LeBlack only ever has—had—two kinds of guests: conspiracy theory nut jobs and people he could bully and try to humiliate. After that Emerald City Psychic Fair..." Elvira chook her head. "It was all I could do not to slap his face when I saw him."

"What happened there?"

The psychic's head drooped, and she sighed deeply. When she looked up, her blue-green eyes were sad. "He invited himself. Claire, the person who was running it, thought it might be a good opportunity to get the word out when he offered to come to the fair and do a live show."

"What did he do?"

Elvira's face darkened and her eyes flashed. "He brought these rough-looking guys with him, and they intimidated the customers into leaving, then he picked verbal fights with random vendors. It was a disaster. And after he bad-mouthed not only the event, but specific people there, it was hard to get customers to come back. Claire managed to hold on, because she owned the property, but I lost the house I was renting. I had to move in with my sister. I bet there are many people in Houston who'll be raising a glass to his demise."

"Sounds like you'll be one of them."

"I don't drink, Detective Donovan."

PC raised her hands defensively. "I wasn't trying to imply that you would celebrate his death, just that it solved some problems for you."

"I have never wished a man dead, but I have read some obituaries with great pleasure."

"Mark Twain?"

"Clarence Darrow, actually. It's a common misattribution."

PC wracked her brain for something to say.

Elvira licked her lips and laughed softly. "You made a lot of assumptions about me, based on my appearance, didn't you? Nose piercing and crazy hair, I must be a high school dropout? Corset and leggings, maybe a stripper?"

The detective shifted her feet. "Well… I don't usually—"

"But you did this time. Why don't you ask me how I got into this line of work?"

"Okay. How did you get into this line of work?"

"Glad you asked. I was an attorney for ten years. Worked five of those at a Fortune 500. I had a job many people dream about, but it was killing me. I had no outlet for my creative side, not at work, anyway. I felt a little more… desiccated every day. One morning I woke up and couldn't decide if I should go to work or kill myself. I quit that day. Sold my West U house and brand-new Mercedes, and never looked back."

"But how did you get into Tarot reading?"

"I make jewelry, and I went on a crafting retreat. One of the ladies there brought her cards and did readings for everybody. She had a gorgeous deck. I loved the pictures, so I bought one for myself, and the rest…" Elvira shrugged. "I do a little freelance legal work from time to time to cover the bills, but I never want to go back to Corporate America."

"You could sue LeBlack for a lot of money, if he was defaming your character."

"First of all, I'm a contract attorney, not a trial lawyer. Second, slander is *really* hard to prove in court, even if it's recorded. Harm is very open to interpretation. But if I'd realized he was going to be here, I'd have rescheduled. He was… not my favorite person."

"So why did you share a vape cartridge with him?"

"He kept begging and wouldn't take no for an answer. I didn't want to make a scene in the jury room—my freelance work pays the bills when I have a slow month for readings or jewelry. I figured if I gave him the cartridge, he'd go away."

"And then Brady came over with the coffee. You could have left then."

Elvira laughed. "Watching Brady force LeBlack to call him 'Dr. Michaels' was too entertaining. I was enjoying watching him squirm."

PC snapped the cap back on her pen. "Well, I think that's it for now. Thanks for taking the time."

"Sure."

The detective turned and searched for the lady in the hot pink shawl. She wasn't difficult to find—the garment drew PC's eyes like magnets. She was still sitting on the front row, pale blue yarn in her lap.

Art attached himself to PC's side like a tick. "So what's the story? Did she do it?"

The detective wished she had a can of Doyle repellent. "I don't think so. Can we talk in a little bit, after I speak with this lady in pink?"

Art sighed loudly. A few people turned to look. "I'll wait for you here."

"Thank you."

PC made her way over to her target.

The detective paused as if she'd only just noticed the crochet project. "Hey, what are you making?"

The lady looked up with drowsy eyes. "Baby blanket. Got a grandson coming next month." She held up the textured blanket.

"That's gorgeous!"

The detective sat down. "Shame about that guy at the back."

The woman nodded. "Yes. It happens a lot, though. My husband had a heart attack on the golf course. Couldn't save him. Thirty-eight years we were married, now it's gone to dust."

"I'm sorry for your loss, ma'am."

The crochet hook resumed bobbing in and out of the yarn. PC watched her hands for a few moments before she realized the ring was missing.

PC crossed her legs. "Must get caught on the yarn."

"What does?"

"Your ring. The one you said snagged on everything."

The crochet stopped. "What are you talking about?"

"Earlier, when you dropped a piece of paper? LeBlack picked it up for you and got scratched by your ring."

"Have you been smoking wacky tobacky? That didn't happen."

Sure. Maybe it was some other old lady in an uber-pink shawl that scratched him. "Okay."

"I've been sitting here, minding my own business this whole time. I got six rows done."

"Are you saying you came in, did your paperwork and have been crocheting ever since?"

She looked at PC as if the detective had just failed an IQ test. "Pretty much. I only took a short break when Alice came by."

"Oh? And who's Alice?"

"You sure have a lot of questions, missy."

PC gave a good-natured chuckle. "Sorry. I'm a detective, and I was just trying to sort out the story of what happened to Mr. LeBlack before they unlocked the doors. My name is Sergeant Donovan, but you can call me PC."

"What does that mean? Politically Correct?"

"Primrose. My first name is Primrose."

The woman arched an eyebrow. Finally, she said, "If this is official, I suppose I can tell you my name. It's on the paperwork, anyway." She nodded her head to the front desk. "Savannah Turner. Mrs. Turner to you."

"Yes, ma'am. Mrs. Turner. Would you tell me about Alice?"

"She's my age, maybe a little younger. Stopped by and asked me about this baby afghan. I commented on her shawl, and she gave it to me."

"She gave you this pink shawl?"

"Are you impaired? What did I just say?"

PC bit back a retort. "When did this happen?"

"Oh, after we got herded in here like a bunch of feedlot cattle."

"Do you see Alice anywhere?"

Mrs. Turner's head turned as she searched each row. She had to turn sideways to see the chairs right behind her. At last, she shook her head. "Well, don't that beat all. She isn't here."

Chapter 7

How GOOD IS *your vision, Savannah? Alice has to be here some-where.* "I'm sure she's around. Do you remember what she was wearing? Maybe I can find her."

Savanah scratched her chin. "You know, I was so focused on the shawl I didn't take much note of anything else. I believe she had on a dress or a skirt. I think there was a print, could have been floral."

"But you could identify her if you saw her, right?"

"Of course. Well… I think so."

Great. Does Alice really exist, or is Savannah just doing a terrible job of lying? "What color was her hair?"

"I'm not sure. It was pulled back, and she was wearing a scarf over it."

PC picked at the skin on her thumbnail. "What color was the scarf?"

"The color?" Savannah looked at her yarn. "It was blue, like in those vacation posters you see of the Yucatan."

That much they could agree on. PC clearly remembered the blue scarf above the lurid shawl. "I see. Let me just get this straight in my head. You were sitting here knitting—"

"Crocheting."

"Crocheting. And a woman, a little younger than you, with a bright blue scarf on her head and wearing a skirt, or perhaps a dress, with what might have been a floral print, comes up to you, admires your blanket, and gives you this hot pink shawl. Is that correct?"

Savannah sniffed. "You don't have to make me sound like an idiot."

"I'm sorry. I'm not accusing you of not telling the truth, but it does seem a little… far-fetched. Do you think it's common for people to give away clothing to random strangers?"

"You'll have to ask the folks at Goodwill."

PC ran a hand through her short hair. "That's different, don't you think?" She gestured toward the shawl. "May I see this?"

With a scowl, Savannah handed the radioactive wrap over.

The thing was so bright PC wished she hadn't left her sunglasses in the car. Shocking pink and neon orange flowers with electric lime centers clumped together in three long rows of blinding acrylic. Grudgingly, PC accepted the idea that someone could fail to remember anything about the person wearing it when confronted with this monstrosity. She wasn't sure she could recall the woman's face clearly herself.

Stories about cursed objects that must be given away before midnight on a certain day popped into her head.

She examined the garment more closely. The stitches were bumpy, like the work Savannah was doing now, so it looked crocheted. The detective turned it over and found a tag from *Charlene's Handmade* and a URL for an Etsy shop. She took a picture. Did someone named Alice really buy this hideous thing? Was either Alice or Charlene colorblind?

Savannah extended her hand.

PC handed the eye-breaking shawl back to her. "Alright. I'll look around and see if I can find Alice. Thank you."

Savanah settled the wrap around her shoulders and picked up her baby afghan.

The detective took a few steps up the aisle and scanned the jury pool.

"How about now? You ready to talk about the case now?" Art loomed hopefully to her left.

He was a persistent dude. PC had to give him credit for that. He reminded her of Cordite when he wanted his butt scratched. There wasn't a good way to stop his harassment, other than scratching his itch. Art seemed to be the same. Even if PC had the ability to ask uniforms to remove him from the scene, there was no place for him to be removed to, not while they were in lockdown. If she made a big scene with Art, people might be less willing to talk to her. Perhaps if she gave him something to do to get him out of her hair…

"I'm looking for someone. Can you help me find her?"

His eyes almost bugged out of his head. "Is it the killer?"

PC looked around, then leaned over to whisper to him. "Maybe."

Art coughed. "Okay. Give me the BOLO. What are we looking out for?"

"Okay. Don't make it obvious that you're searching for something. Just be casual. And whatever you do, do *not* speak to her, understood? We don't want to tip her off, okay?"

He nodded eagerly. "Got it. I always wanted to be involved in a genuine investigation."

No one appeared to be eavesdropping. "The woman will be middle aged, wearing a dress or skirt with a pattern, possibly floral. Her hair was pulled back and covered with a blue scarf earlier, but she could have taken off the scarf and let her hair down."

"In case she wants to look different, right?"

PC nodded. *If Alice exists, and if she has something to hide.*

"I'm on it!"

Hope I haven't created a monster. She jumped as the phone in her pocket vibrated. Finally, an answer from Rocky. "I couldn't remember if Hazel got her hay on the ground or in the feeder thing. Left a flake on the ground for her. Off to work."

PC glanced at her FlitBit. He should have been at work two hours ago, so it seemed either the text had taken forever to arrive or Rocky slept in. And Rocky never slept in, not even on Sundays.

She replied, "That's fine. Thank you!" and wondered if she would arrive back home before the text reached her brother.

Then she noticed Toby at the back of the room. He was sitting in one of the chairs that marked off LeBlack's body. He appeared to be texting like his life depended on it. *Good luck with that, buddy.*

Still, something about his demeanor held her attention. He would type, pause, type some more, as if he was having a conversation.

You idiot, she chided herself. Of course, he can text and probably call. As an employee, Toby has access to the building's secure, internal Wi-Fi. He was unlikely to give her the password to connect, but he might send a message or two for her. Wouldn't hurt to ask—the worst he would do was say no.

PC noted that Cheryl at the front desk was also busy texting. *Were they messaging each other?* The detective approached Toby and stood quietly until he finished typing.

"Hey, Toby. I was wondering—"

He held up a hand. "Now's not the time."

"Oh?"

"It's getting rough out there. We're fine, don't worry. These idiots don't realize that Albert Jackson isn't even here. He's still in the county lockup, attending his hearing over a video feed."

There was an edge to his voice that hadn't been there earlier. There was something else that hadn't been there earlier: a faint, bitter, acrid smell that clung to both crime victims and offenders in the interrogation room who were looking down the barrel of a life sentence, if not death row.

Fear.

The chill of it embraced PC's gut and its gangly fingers slithered up her spine. She swallowed hard, but played along with his reassurances.

"Someone should tell them. Then they could go down there and be funneled straight into the tank."

"Not enough room."

How many are out there?

Toby bowed his head to type on his phone, and PC turned back to the pool of jurors who milled around aimlessly, unaware of the potential danger they were in. And yet there wasn't a thing she could do about it. The only contribution she could possibly make at this time was to continue her probe into LeBlack's death.

If it was natural causes, so be it. If not, a list of suspects, and with any luck, evidence, would be immensely helpful to the official investigators. They'd do their own investigation, anyway, but she might be able to save them some time. If it was even a homicide. She'd never live it down if she convinced them to investigate a heart attack.

PC closed her eyes for a long moment. *Focus on what you can control.*

She scanned the crowd. Art was surreptitiously taking notes. Did that mean he'd found Alice? PC would also search. It wasn't like she had anything else to do. Except for one thing.

The detective sent a text. "Hey, Felicity. If you have a minute, I need your help. No internet here. Could you check the web for information re: Mack LeBlack and any of the following? Art Doyle (60s), Savannah Turner (60s), Dr. Brady Michaels (30s, biologist), Elvira Ravenstone (30s, psychic), Peter Smitherson (40s), and Dallas Papadopoulos (30s, pottery business). Your chance to be an investigator! TY"

It may take hours to get a response, so the sooner she sent it, the better.

Now, which one of these ladies is Alice?

PC casually made her way around the room, looking into the trash cans for a discarded scarf or other clothing item.

First bin, near the front desk. Nothing but papers.

Second, back left corner. Papers and coffee cups.

Third, back right corner. Papers, coffee cups, and something colorful underneath the Styrofoam debris.

She tipped the plastic receptacle over with her foot. People turned toward the noise.

The detective sheepishly hung her head. "I'm such a klutz. Really need to watch where I'm going."

She knelt to clean up the mess, wishing she still had the glove Toby had given her. The color she'd glimpsed was from a post card advertising discount dental services. Too bad true crime wasn't just pushpins and string. Her hand was sticky now from the coffee residue in the cups. *Yuck.* She should check if Cheryl had some desk spray or something.

By the time she got to the front desk, Cheryl had a package of baby wipes out. "Find what you were looking for?"

PC took one of the moist towelettes and shook her head. "No. False alarm. But thanks for the clean-up."

"What *were* you looking for, anyway?"

"A scarf." The detective's eyes fell on the stack of jury summonses on Cheryl's desk.

"A scarf?"

"Yeah. A woman who talked to LeBlack right before he died was reported as wearing one, but nobody has one now. Do you mind if I look through that paperwork to confirm a name?"

"I can't let you do that, but if you tell me the name, I'll tell you if they've checked in."

"Alice. Don't have a last name."

While Cheryl flipped through the pages, PC looked for her accomplice. Art was standing near a clump of women, taking notes.

Well, that's not creepy at all.

The sound of paper shuffling stopped, and PC turned her attention back to the front desk.

Cheryl tapped the upright papers on the desk to straighten them. "There are two Alices. A Poe and a Lewis. Does that help?"

"A lot, thank you."

Two Alices. Is one a killer? Or are both coincidental, inadvertently swept up by a lie? She began her own search.

PC turned to the group of women Art was studying. A woman with grey hair and unlined skin with a very short, sculpted haircut. Her brown dress had a slightly lighter brown design on it. *Floral or paisley?* PC couldn't tell from here.

Another woman sat alone reading a book, about midway down the second column of chairs, close to the wall. Her salt-and-pepper hair hung in a braid past her waist. A dark purple skirt populated with pink and white roses pooled around her legs.

A third potential Alice sat near the back, in the first column of chairs. Her shoulder-length blonde hair sported a blue streak at the front and was held in a low ponytail at the back by an ornate metal barrette. An abstract pattern flowed across her aqua skirt.

A fourth woman might fit the bill. Sitting near the front, her shiny, jet black hair was slicked into an austere bun. She caught PC looking at her and glared back, her hawkish features exuding menace, counter to the gentle vine and leaf pattern on her green dress.

Another lady stood near the door, tapping on her phone. Her brown hair was caught in an elegant French braid that terminated in a black lace bow at the back of her neck. A subtle silver damask pattern covered her black sheath dress. She was talking to Elvira, and PC wondered if she was getting a psychic reading.

Most of the other women wore pants, although there were a few dresses and skirts in stripes, polka dots, and solids. She'd consider them, if none of these five turned out to be Alice. Elvira moved over a few feet and started an animated conversation with a small knot of people.

No time like the present.

The lady with the French braid and black dress didn't look up when PC got within a few feet of her and called, "Alice?"

Maybe she didn't hear over the chatter? The detective cleared her throat to try again.

A loud boom sounded. Ambient chatter died. Another boom.

The lights snapped off, plunging the jury room into utter darkness.

Chapter 8

"EVERYBODY STAY STILL! Remain calm."

That was Toby's voice.

A grunt immediately preceded the sound of an object sliding across the floor.

"Stay where you are! The emergency lights should come on shortly." Toby again.

As if on command, the floodlights at the door and the back of the room popped on and cast a sallow glow immediately beneath themselves, scarcely illuminating the room's edges. It made PC think of a nightclub, although she hadn't been in one in decades. Light enough to see that you were dancing with someone, dark enough you probably wouldn't recognize them in full daylight.

The fear in the room felt like a living thing, its breath moistened by the exhalations of the jury pool and warmed by the heat of their bodies. The collective release of adrenalin fueled its pounding pulse, and its scimitar talons could rip reason and order to shreds in the beat of a heart.

With a clang and a groan, the AC lumbered to life and the fluorescent lights blazed, leaving people squinting and blinking.

PC hurried to the back of the room to speak with Toby. She found him, surrounded by a ring of panicky people.

"What is happening?"

"When will we get out of here?"

"Are we going to die?"

They peppered him with questions, giving him no time to answer.

The detective put two fingers in her mouth and made a piercing whistle. The entire room went silent.

"As you were." PC said as loudly as she could without shouting.

The conversations resumed, but at a much-reduced decibel.

Toby's eyes flashed gratitude to PC. He spread his hands in front of him, pushing downward, as he spoke to the people surrounding him. "I need you to settle down. We are safe in here. No one has breached the building. The flood doors to the tunnels are shut. They tried to cut our power, but we have our own generators. I know it's scary, y'all, but we're going to be just fine."

One woman didn't seem convinced and burst into tears. Several people moved to comfort her. A nervous man left to pace the aisleway. A few others stood, in various poses of defiance, with hard eyes and clenched jaws.

"Excuse us for a minute." PC led Toby as far away from them as she could get—up against the wall next to LeBlack's body. "Okay," she whispered. "What's really going on?"

"They've called the DPS state troopers for backup. The mayor is on the phone with the governor to request the National Guard. These guys are bad news. Not our normal protestors. But we are safe in here. Don't doubt that."

"I don't doubt we're well-protected, but these people are scared, and scared people do crazy-stupid things."

Toby stroked his chin. "You have any ideas on how to unscare them?"

A song PC didn't recognize burst from Toby's pocket.

He fumbled for his phone. "Hey, baby... yeah, I'm fine... I know... I know... We're safe, really... Yeah. I have to go. I love you. Bye." Toby's lips curved into a momentary approximation of a smile. "My wife. She's watching the news."

PC nodded. Then she tapped her top lip. "Music soothes he savage beast, right?"

"You expecting a DJ?"

"No. But there is a PA system. I'm going to talk to Cheryl."

As the detective made her way to the front desk, Art fell into line, trotting at her heels like a hungry puppy. "I've got a lot to tell you!"

"Great. I'm happy to hear it. But I have to take care of something first."

PC put on a smile that was brighter than she felt. "Hey, Cheryl. Is there a way to play music over the PA system? I was thinking something calm, soothing... maybe classical? Smooth jazz? Something like that?"

"That's a good idea. A really good idea. I know just the thing."

"Okay, now can we talk?" Art touched her elbow.

PC squelched the urge to smack him. "Okay." She looked around. There was an area at the front with no chairs that appeared to be devoid of possible Alices. She gestured in that direction. He followed.

"Okay, Art. What did you find out?"

The beginning notes of *Eine Klein Nachtmusik* leaped from the speakers of the PA system.

He pulled out his notes with a self-satisfied smirk. "I found eight ladies who could be Alice, based on your description."

Eight? Did I really miss three? "Tell me about them."

"Alright, so the first one is the redhead in the black and white dress, sitting with the guy in the red shirt." He turned his head and PC's eyes followed his.

She bit the inside of her cheek. "I guess technically, any design on fabric is a print, at least most of the time, but I don't think geometric patterns, like stripes, polka dots, or checks, should count as prints. I mean you'd say, 'I have a floral print skirt,' but you'd never say, 'I have a stripe print skirt,' now would you? You'd just say a striped skirt, right?"

"I wouldn't say any of those things," Art sulked. "But I suppose I see your point." He grudgingly crossed three names off his list.

"So, now what have you got?"

"Suspect number one." Art clicked his pen. "She's standing not too far from the door. Very short grey hair. Brown dress, with some slightly lighter brown patterns. I can't quite tell what it's supposed to be."

Good. I noted the same one. "Alright. Next?"

Art craned his neck, searching the room. "There she is." He nodded to the woman in the black dress with the French braid.

Another hit. "Yep."

Art grinned. "What about the blonde over there with the blue in her hair?"

"I think she fits."

"What about the one in the back corner in the purple skirt with flowers on it?"

PC nodded. "With the really long braid?"

"That's her." Art looked around the room, squinting. "There's the last one. Do you see her, about halfway down the first section of chairs, in the green dress?"

"Black hair, looks like she'd tear your face off?"

Art chuckled. "Yes. Now, are we going to go talk to them?"

"*We* are not going to do anything. I'll talk to them. But first, I need to send a text before I forget."

The would-be investigator frowned.

PC pulled out her phone to text Felicity. "Me again. Hope I'm not being too much trouble. Could you search for Alice Poe and Alice Lewis to see if they're connected to Mack LeBlack in any way? TY!"

The detective turned back to the padfoot. "Okay, Art. Did you happen to notice whether any of these women were wearing rings?"

"Rings?"

"Yes. The person we're looking for was wearing a ring that scratched Mr. LeBlack. She said there was a missing stone and the empty setting snagged on everything."

Art drooped. "I didn't look for rings. You just told me about the hair and dress."

"I'm sorry. I should have mentioned it. It's one of those anniversary settings, with a row of diamonds, all the same size, across the top. I think there were seven, but I suppose there could have been five."

Sadness swept across his face, but he said nothing.

"You okay? What's wrong, Art?"

"It's fine." He shrugged one shoulder. "My parents would have been married fifty years this month. My father. He was killed on the freeway fifteen years ago."

"I'm really sorry to hear that."

"Mother's never been the same. We both really miss him."

He looked miserable.

She wanted to tell him she'd lost her father, too. At a young age, when she'd needed him so much. How that kind of wound never really healed, although the scar is both tough and tender to the touch. But she didn't. He didn't need to know about her father, and he already knew the other things.

PC squeezed his shoulder. "Did you want to take a break for a while?"

"No. I need to keep busy. This will pass—it always does."

"Losing someone is hard. Sometimes little things just hit you like a falling piano."

Trey Donovan wasn't the only person PC had lost. Mike, her fiancé had been killed shortly before the wedding in a car crash.

They'd fought.

Something dumb—the catering menu.

She'd gotten the call in the middle of the night.

Better hurry.

And then she'd felt crushed by fate, as if under the weight of a falling piano. Mike had always said that. He told her that 'a ton of bricks' was cliché.

PC shook her head. *I can't just sit here and wallow with Art. Have to keep busy.*

The detective forced a smile. "Alright. Let's get to work. You go check for rings and then we'll go from there."

Art rolled his eyes like a surly teen but set off on his mission.

Elvira Ravenstone and Brady Michaels were chatting again, standing about three quarters of the way to the back of the room. After LeBlack sent his flying monkeys after her, she'd gotten death threats and lost her home. She definitely had reason to hate LeBlack. Michaels was appalled by LeBlack's unsound environmental policies, and enraged about him encouraging his listeners to forage endangered turtle eggs, but was it enough to kill?

Dallas Papadopoulos flipped through a magazine in the second row, near the far wall. He stood to lose his home-based pottery business if the zoning ordinance that LeBlack was pushing succeeded. Otherwise, he was a big fan. Unless it turned out he had anger management issues or some type of disordered personality, he probably wouldn't have killed his hero.

It took a moment to locate Peter Smitherson. His mother was still suffering from a head injury since she'd been hit by a red-light runner—after the talk show host had campaigned to get traffic cameras removed. And LeBlack had bullied him in the jury pool room. Stronger suspect than Papadopoulos.

Savannah Turner, the crochet lady. Yarn and afghan in her lap, she sat in the second row working on her project as if she were at home. Strangest suspect—either the best or the worst. She denied knowing who LeBlack was, yet she was seen wearing that hideous pink shawl and scratching him with a ring. Well, a woman wearing that eyesore approached the decedent. *Maybe everyone was so focused on it that nobody paid attention to her face?* Savannah claims the shawl was given to her by someone named Alice, whom she couldn't locate in the room.

The mysterious Alice. Two Alices have checked in for jury duty. Could one of them be the killer? She'd have to locate Alice to find out, and that would prove whether Savannah was lying or telling the truth.

"None of them."

PC was jolted out of her puzzling by Art's voice. "What?"

He gestured dramatically with his hands. "None of them were wearing rings."

"Okay then. Let's just pick one and start."

She'd decided to try the lady in the brown dress first. She was the closest. On the way, they passed Savannah, her crochet hook flying in and out of the yarn. But it wasn't the baby blanket that caught PC's eye. She stopped and Art nearly plowed into her.

"Hey! What's up with that?" he complained at her.

PC ignored him, her eyes locked on a wisp of greenish blue. In passing, she'd noticed that the bag hanging on the back of Savannah's chair wasn't zipped all the way.

Something bright blue peeked out of it.

"Mrs. Turner? Is that your purse?" PC pointed to the handbag.

The other woman looked over her shoulder. "Yes."

"Do you remember what color scarf the woman who gave you the shawl was wearing?"

Savannah scrunched up her face. "Pretty sure it was blue."

"Is it the same blue as the scarf in your purse?"

"What?" The crocheter twisted around in her chair to grab the bag. Color drained from her face as she saw the aquamarine tail of the scarf jutting out of the unzipped portion.

She yanked the zipper open and tugged the scarf out of the bag. It was wedged in tightly and when it popped out a blue nitrile glove and the fancy ring that had been wrapped inside scattered onto the floor.

Chapter 9

"THAT'S NOT MINE!" Savannah leaned over to pick the items up.

PC grabbed her arm. "No! Don't touch that."

A few people turned around, then went back to their whispered conversations.

The detective pulled out her phone. "I'm going to take a few pictures." She snapped the objects, the purse, and the chair.

Art cocked his eyebrow, as if he were a film noir detective. "What are you trying to hide?"

"I'm not trying to hide anything. That stuff doesn't belong to me!"

"It was in your purse!"

"Whoa, whoa, whoa," PC broke in. "It wasn't there when I talked to Mrs. Turner earlier. Art? Would you go back there and get me at least 3 sheets of paper and that stapler?"

He gave her a sarcastic little salute and stomped off.

PC put a chair over the spilled items, so no one stepped on them. "So, Mrs. Turner? If those things don't belong to you, how do you suppose they got in your purse?"

"How should I know? Somebody could have stuffed them in when the lights were out. But why? Why would someone do that?"

"If Mr. LeBlack died of natural causes, then that's an excellent question. If someone killed him, for example, with a ring smeared with some type of contact poison, they might want to get rid of the evidence, right?"

Or call attention to the evidence and pretend that someone planted it on them to try to derail the investigation.

The metal crochet hook clattered to the floor. "Why me?"

"If I were guessing, I'd guess they think one older woman in a garish pink shawl looks very much like another. Perhaps the dramatic shawl was a distraction, so nobody paid attention to the woman's face."

Savannah laughed. "You're old enough to know that no one pays attention to an older woman's face, anyway. After forty, women become invisible. We're like ghosts, haunting our own lives."

PC shifted her weight. "Now Mrs. Turner…"

"Could you pick up that hook for me?" Savannah pointed to the blue implement that had rolled under the chair next to her.

The detective retrieved the hook and handed it back.

"Thank you."

A glowering Art returned, smelling of peppermint, with the paper and stapler. PC still had the pen she'd used earlier in her bag, so she wrote out the location found and a description of each item. She rolled two sheets of paper into a tight tube and used it to push each item into its own makeshift envelope, then stapled them closed.

Art stood and watched, smacking his gum during the entire process.

"I'm going to put these with the rest of the evidence. If you remember anything, I'll be around."

Savannah nodded.

PC headed to where Toby was guarding LeBlack's body.

Art dogged her steps. "Well? Are you going to tell him to arrest her?"

"What? No."

"Why not? She sure looks suspicious to me."

PC stopped. "Does she strike you as being stupid?"

"Stupid? Cranky, perhaps, but no, I wouldn't say stupid."

"Good. So, if you had a striking blue scarf, with the murder weapon and some gloves that probably contain your DNA all wrapped up in it, would you leave the end sticking out of your pocket for someone who was specifically looking for a blue scarf to see?"

Art pursed his lips. "Just because she's not dumb doesn't mean she's good at being a killer."

"Maybe. But we have to locate Alice. If Mrs. Turner's story that Alice gave her the pink shawl is true, then it seems reasonable she could be the killer, although there are at least four other people in the room who had a grudge against Mr. LeBlack. According to the paperwork, there are two actual Alices here. Alice may be a lie, or she may be a murderer. That's what we've got to find out."

Pop! The small bubble between Art's teeth deflated. "Or it could be natural causes."

"That, too. Alice might just be the type of person who would give someone the shawl off her back, and she wasn't trying to get rid of incriminating evidence at all."

Art popped his gum again.

The detective continued on her evidence delivery mission.

What task could she send Art on now to keep him from being underfoot? All that popping and smacking was getting under her skin.

Toby stared vacantly at his cell phone in one hand, the other hand on his hip.

"What's the status?" PC asked quietly.

Toby shook himself. "Rioters set fire to the little park outside, but the fire department was able to use a chopper to put it out. DPS is on the way with MRAPs. The Guard's on standby."

"MRAPs? What's that?" Art asked loudly.

Toby looked at PC, then to her companion. "Kind of armored personnel carrier. Mine Resistant Ambush Protected."

The detective scratched her chin. "They can't use… dispersants?"

"Those guys came prepared. They've got face shields and gas masks. And they're armed to the teeth. City's trying to keep people from getting killed, but so far, their de-escalation plan hasn't worked as well as they'd hoped."

PC swallowed. Her mouth was dry and her throat tight. If they over-ran the building, they would probably go upstairs, to the courtrooms to look for Albert Jackson, not come into the basement where the jury pool was.

Probably.

She didn't just need to distract Art—she also needed to focus on something else: finding Alice. PC set the new paper evidence envelopes on the chair with the others.

Art's jaw moved, and the gum made a wet squelch against his teeth.

The detective snatched up a piece of typing paper and folded it in half, then opened it in front of Art's face. "Spit it out."

"What?"

"Your gum. Spit. It. Out. You are leaning on my last nerve with that noise."

His lips gathered into a pout before he spat the grey wad into the paper.

PC folded the open sides together. Her phone vibrated. She set the used gum down on one of the chairs and pulled out her device.

A reply from Felicity. "Found some socials for six Arthur Doyles. Nothing special. No mention of LeBlack on any of them."

PC replied, "Thank you!"

She waited a few moments, hoping for more information, but her phone remained silent. *Oh, well. Back to Alice.*

The officer sagged onto a chair. His breathing was shallow.

PC knew the feeling. "You okay, Toby? Anything we can get you?"

He shook his head, then stopped. "Actually, I was supposed to go home an hour ago. Haven't eaten since 2:30 this morning. Starting to get the shakes. Could you get me a protein bar from Cheryl? She always has a box in her desk."

"Of course." PC turned to Art. "Would you please go and ask Cheryl for a protein bar?"

"But—"

"I thought you wanted to help."

He slunk off down the aisleway.

PC's phone vibrated again. Felicity. "Several Savannah Turners. One has an Instagram and an Etsy shop. No connection I can find to LeBlack."

"TY! Name of shop?"

Again, PC waited. Silence from the phone. *Better find a potential Alice before Art gets back.* The lady in the brown dress with the close-cropped grey hair sat about four rows away, reading a paperback.

The detective made her way over. Brown Dress Alice dog-eared a page, closed the book, and applied lip balm.

The cover had a picture of a half-naked man carrying a sword. A castle rose from the mist in the background, and a dragon approached it from the left. Pink script revealed the author's name as Portia L'Amour.

Brown Dress Alice put away the plastic tube and re-opened the book.

PC took her opportunity and sat down. "Is that the latest Portia L'Amour?"

The woman looked up, and her jaw clenched slightly and released. "It's not *the* latest, but one of the latest." Her eyes returned to the pages in front of her.

"Oh. Sorry to bother you. My sister loves those books, and her birthday's coming up next week. My name's PC, by the way." She held out a hand.

Brown Dress Alice took PC's hand limply. "I'm Marguerite. If you don't mind…?" She gestured to her book.

"Oh! Sure thing. If I could ask you just one more question?"

"What is it?"

"There was a lady with a pink shawl earlier. I thought it might have been you." PC cast her eyes to Marguerite's chair and the surrounding floor.

"No. It wasn't me. I never wear pink."

"I'll bet blue looks great on you. You know, that bright Caribbean blue?"

Marguerite pursed her lips. "I typically wear earth tones. But thank you for the unsolicited fashion advice."

PC nodded. Pushing further would only alienate the woman. "Okay. Well, enjoy your book."

The detective got up and left, searching for the next possible Alice. She paused to write down Marguerite's name and description before she moved on.

The blonde woman with the blue streak in her hair was the next closest.

"What did you find out?" Art had returned from his errand of mercy and now stood too close to her.

"Not much. She says her name's Marguerite, and she doesn't wear pink or blue."

"So, who's next?"

PC startled when her phone vibrated. The messages from Felicity were coming thick and fast, now. "Dr. Brady Michaels, environmental biologist for state. Accused of belonging to eco-terrorist group, he denies it, no connection ever proven. Public spats with LeBlack and others. Going to make b'fast now. Back later."

The detective checked her FlitBit. It was 10:38. She really hoped that Felicity ate a late breakfast, and there weren't hours between the texts PC sent and replies she got. That seemed to be the case with Rocky, but it also could have been that he was on his way to work.

"Anything interesting?"

PC shrugged, desperate to come up with another fool's errand for Art.

"Who are we talking to next?"

"Um… you know what would really be helpful?"

He frowned, clearly expecting a menial task. "What?"

"I'd like you to check the trash cans. You don't have to be obvious or dig around, just look inside and see if there seems to be anything unusual. Also, my pen is out of ink, and I'm low on paper."

His eyes narrowed, and if he were trying to sus out her intentions.

PC gave him a benevolent smile. "You said you wanted to be helpful, and you loved true crime. Welcome to the glamorous world of investigation."

He turned without comment and started toward the back of the room.

Hopefully, that'll be at least one Alice's worth, two if I'm really lucky.

Her phone rumbled in her pocket. *Well, well, well. Speaking of luck...*

Another text from Felicity. "Elvira Ravenstone. Shop set on fire after LeBlack featured a psychic fair on his show. Her sister seriously burned but survived. Lawsuit that didn't go anywhere. Legal name Alice Lewis."

Chapter 10

My, my, my. We have our first actual Alice. Why did she hold out on me about her sister and the fire when we talked earlier? PC looked around for Elvira.

The woman with the mermaid hair leaned against the far wall, talking to a tall, lanky young man. She could have put a scarf over her head and handed off the shawl, but Savannah had said the woman was around her age. No way Elvira could pass for a woman twice her years, not without extensive makeup, and when would she have been able to take it off?

Still, PC couldn't cross her off the list of suspects. There were some powerful reasons she might want revenge on LeBlack. And she was a confirmed Alice.

The detective still had to find the other Alice, though.

The blonde with the blue streak was still the closest of the potential Alices. Sitting in about the middle of the first section of chairs, she appeared to be playing a game on her tablet.

There were two empty chairs behind Blue Streak Alice, so PC made her way to one.

She stole a look at the screen in the woman's lap before sitting down. "That game looks interesting. What's it called?"

Blue Streak Alice held up the tablet for PC to get a better look. "Sunfrost Mountain. I usually play it at night, before I go to sleep, but I really need to take my mind off this whole situation. I can't believe we're locked in a room with a dead body and there's a pitchforks-and-torches mob outside."

"I know. Wish I'd thought of bringing something like that."

"Mobile games. Aren't they the best? You can get a version of this for your phone."

"Too bad I can't get a signal."

Blue Streak Alice nodded sympathetically. "Download it when we get out of here. You'll be glad you did."

"Maybe I'll do that. I can always use a good de-stressor."

The blonde turned sideways in her chair. "My name is Devon, by the way."

"I'm PC."

Devon put her tablet back in her lap. "Have you lived here long? I just moved here from Chicago six months ago. Still trying to find my way around."

"Really? I've lived here most of my life. What part of town are you in?"

"Energy Corridor. You?"

"My house is in the Heights."

"Easy commute here for you, then."

PC pulled her chair forward a little. "Yeah, not too bad. Energy Corridor's on the bleeding edge of West Houston. I'll bet you spend a lot of time in the car, listening to the radio."

"Not too much radio. Podcasts, mostly, but some NPR."

PC feigned surprise. "Ohhh." She tilted her head to the back corner of the room. "So you don't know who that is?"

"Who?"

"The, uh, dead guy."

Devon shrugged. "No idea."

"He's—was—a local celebrity. Had a long-running radio talk show. Ran for mayor a few times, but never came anywhere near winning. Kinda controversial."

Devon cocked her head. "Aren't they always?"

"Yeah…"

The tablet in Devon's lap played a few notes of music. "Sorry. I have to harvest my pomegranates before the harp-bees get them."

"Sure. It was nice talking to you."

Devon began tapping the screen and dragging her finger on her device. PC waited a minute or two before getting up. *Two Alices down, three to go.*

She made a few quick notes and scanned for her next subject. Angry Alice perched on her chair four rows down across the aisle.

"I got you three pens. And more paper. I didn't see anything that didn't look like garbage in the trash cans." Art's nasal voice grated on PC's ears like metal on metal.

"Thank you." *Now where do I send you?*

Art shoved the office supplies into her hands. "Yeah. So, listen. While I was back there, I talked to Brady Michaels for a minute."

"Did you, now?" *Hope he hasn't spooked him.*

His look was sullen. "You might want to hear this."

"Okay. What did he have to say?"

Art stepped closer to PC, invading her space. "He said that somebody started a petition to get him fired."

"Let me guess—LeBlack?"

"Not him. But close. His co-host, Troy Lendon."

Huh. "Wonder why he didn't mention that. Michaels didn't seem to have any shortage of complaints against LeBlack."

Art spread his hands. "Did the apprentice-troll take it upon himself to do it?"

"Maybe." PC clicked her pen. "But I'd be surprised if the troll and his apprentice didn't keep each other's counsel." She knew she shouldn't talk about a decedent like that, but it seemed the more she found out about Mack LeBlack, the more awful he was. She couldn't allow her dislike for the man to color her fact-finding mission, however.

Art snorted. "Oh, I agree. LeBlack probably put him up to it."

PC glanced over her shoulder in Brady's direction. "I hope his bosses don't take that garbage seriously." She'd like to confirm that, though.

"Yeah. But that's a good reason for him to want to end LeB-lack—cut the head off the snake, and it won't bite you again."

"There's that." Something glittered on Art's shoulder. She reached over and picked it off. "How did you get a paperclip stuck to you?"

"My magnetic personality?" Art grinned.

No, that's not it. A tight semi-smile bent her lips for a moment. She fastened her notes together with the clip, since it was in her hand.

"So what did she have to say?"

"Who?"

He rolled his eyes. "You know who I'm talking about. Blonde Alice in the blue dress with the…" Art stared over PC's shoulder, scowling "… what even is that? Leaves? Feathers?"

"Her name isn't Alice, and she says she just moved here from Chicago. Never heard of LeBlack."

"Well, I'd say that too, if I'd killed him."

"I'm sure you would."

PC pulled out her phone to message Felicity about the petition to fire Brady. Before she could tap on the text icon, the device vibrated.

Another text from Felicity. "This Peter Smitherson?"

A loading wheel spun on the screen. *Can I even get a picture here?*

She waited. The wheel turned. PC set the phone down. A watched document never loads. Nothing she could do until it either came through or timed out.

Art peered at her phone, then back at her. "So which one are we going to talk to next?"

"*We* aren't going to talk to anybody. I will do the talking."

"Like you talked to Brady Michaels and found out there was a petition to get him fired? Oh, wait…"

PC let out a breath. "I don't know why you're trying to pick a fight with me."

"Me? Trying to pick a fight with *you*? You're the one treating me like a child. I don't have to put up with that."

"Okay." PC turned and started walking toward Angry Alice, a smile on her lips.

"Wait!" Art hurried after her. "I'm sorry. You're right. You're the seasoned investigator. I just watch TV. I want to help. Really."

How can I miss you if you won't go away?

"Find a place to park yourself for now."

With a sorrowful sigh, he wilted down onto the chair and looked at her like a dog being left at the groomers.

Angry Alice had moved, and PC ran her eyes around the chamber, looking for her. People in the jury pool had calmed down some, mostly chattering nervously to their neighbors, or wandering around the cavernous room. The fear had decreased from a palpable thing to an undercurrent, but it was still there. A few jurors glanced up at the locked door from time to time as they spoke. Some had books or devices to shut out the world around them.

PC had never been in the jury room before, but she'd been to Jury Plaza many a time. She had a love-hate relationship with the courtroom. As much as she loved getting a conviction, it was also a hard place to be. Knowing someone has been murdered and seeing crime scene photos of the murder are two very different things, and really tough on the victims' loved ones. Describing to the jury, in detail, what had happened to a decedent, knowing their mother was sitting in the front row, was soul-crushing.

She checked her phone to see if the picture had loaded. There, in all its lo-res glory, was a picture of an old car, PC guessed from the 60s or 70s, lovingly restored with fresh candy-apple red paint and a white vinyl top. Gold pinstripes accented the curves of the bodywork.

Standing in front of the car and behind a woman in a wheelchair was Peter Smitherson.

PC replied to Felicity's text. "Yes. That's him. Could you find out if there is a petition to get Dr. Brady Michaels fired from Texas parks dept? TY!"

Now, Angry Alice, where are you?

Chapter 11

ANGRY ALICE SAT on the front row, in front of the desk, with her arms crossed. At first, she appeared to be glowering at Cheryl, who was typing on her computer. Then PC realized that Angry Alice's eyes were unfocused, as if lost in thought.

The detective strolled up to the daydreaming woman and stopped almost a few feet away. "Excuse me? Miss?"

She shook herself and looked up. "Yes?"

"I *love* your dress. Do you mind my asking where you got it?"

Angry Alice looked down at her body, as if she didn't know what clothes she was wearing. "Thank you. My daughter gave it to me. No idea where she got it. Sorry."

PC sat down next to her. "That's a shame. I have a party next weekend that would be absolutely perfect for."

The other woman smiled and her face softened. "I can call her and ask, but she lives in California."

"That might be a little far to go shopping." The detective put a hand on her chest. "I'm PC, by the way."

"It's lovely to meet you, Peasy. I am Rosella Portanova."

"Like Portanova Custom Boots?"

"Exactly like that. My great grandfather opened the first boot-making shop in Houston. 1842. We've been here a while."

"My father had a pair of custom Portanovas. His favorite, not just boots, but shoes in general. It's an honor to make your acquaintance."

Rosella chuckled. "Not me. I don't make the boots." Her eyes sparkled with mirth.

"Well, your family is a Houston treasure."

"Perhaps." Rosella dipped her head. "I would just like to get out of here. If my mother sees this on the news…" She sighed. "She's in her eighties. This won't be good for her heart."

PC was suddenly glad that Rose didn't watch news during the day. "I hope she has something else to do. This hasn't been too bad for us, but it probably looks a lot worse outside. Surely these crazies will leave soon. I'm ready to go home as well."

"It's worse than it could be, having that dead body in the back. I think Mack LeBlack specialized in making people uncomfortable in life and carried on the same way in death."

Does she know him? "Shock Jocks get listeners, I suppose."

"He solicited money from me this morning, and not for the first time. Seems he was getting an exploratory committee together to run for state representative. I told him I wouldn't give him money to run for dog catcher."

Maybe not an Alice, but a hint of a motive? "Yeah. I'd heard he wanted to throw his hat into the political ring."

Rosella pursed her lips. "Not sure who he thought was going to vote for him, though. He was the worst kind of hanger-on. Someone who wangled invites to social events so he could rub shoulders with those who had money to donate to whatever harebrained scheme had had going, then when that inevitably failed, he tried to turn everyone against each other for his own amusement. I'm not saying I'm glad he's dead, but I'm certainly not shedding tears over his maggoty carcass."

So, no love lost there. "Yeah. It seems his personality…"

"Left a lot to be desired?"

"That's what it sounds like. Did you know anyone who did want him dead?"

"I know a number of people who'd delight in dancing on his grave, but actively killing him? No." Rosella shook her head.

"They said it might be a heart attack."

"A heart attack? Don't you have to *have* a heart for that to happen?"

"Touché."

Rosella sighed. "I suppose it's bad luck to speak ill of the dead. Let's change the subject—we need all the good luck we can get today."

PC agreed, and then the two of them chatted about things like animal rescues and environmental policy for almost half an hour. Angry Alice hadn't been angry at all—just bored. Once she'd gotten Rosella talking, the detective found it difficult to extricate herself from the conversation.

When she finally broke free, she was confronted by Art.

"Alice?"

"No. She actually knew LeBlack and couldn't stand him, though."

"Interesting."

"Perhaps."

"Did you two solve the problems of the world?"

PC bristled, but measured her response. "Of course."

Art gazed at the grey carpeting for a moment, then lifted sad puppy eyes to PC. "I miss that."

"Miss what?"

"I told you my dad was killed in an accident, right? Mother was in the same accident. She was badly injured, but survived. Losing my father broke her. She started drinking heavily, then met up with some man at a bar. He took advantage of her, convinced her to marry him, then stole her house out from under her. As soon as he had his paws on the deed, he divorced her."

PC sucked in a breath. "I'm sorry."

"She lives with me now. We used to talk all the time." His shoulders rolled upward. "But now… I don't keep alcohol in the house, and she doesn't have a car. She mostly sits and watches TV. I always put on re-runs of *Night Court* for her. We used to watch it together when I was a kid. It's like she's a shell of her former self. The lights are on, but nobody's home."

"That's a tough place to be."

"Tell me about it." He shook his head. "Look, I'm not trying to cramp your style or interfere in what you're doing. I'm just…"

Lonely. "It's okay, Art. You're doing the right thing, taking care of her."

"Thanks."

"So, which Alice are we going to talk to next?"

PC looked around. Peter Smitherson stood up, swayed, and sat back down again, cradling his head in his hands.

What's up with that?

She rubbed her jaw. "Let's go talk to Smitherson. I'm not sure he's okay."

They made their way over to the nervous man and sat next to him, one on each side.

PC cleared her throat. "Mr. Smitherson? Are you all right?"

Slowly, he raised his head and squinted at her. "Just a headache. Must have stood up too fast, that's all." He rubbed the bruise on the side of his head, which had swollen and darkened considerably since early this morning.

"Mr. Smitherson? Did something happen to you? I noticed that bruise earlier. Did you hit your head?"

He made a choking sob and started rocking back and forth. "She's ruined. She's ruined."

PC and Art looked at each other over the man's bent back. The detective leaned over to be closer to his ear. "Who's ruined?"

"Fabella." His voice broke as he said the name.

"Who is Fabella?"

Smitherson didn't answer. PC raised her head. "Art, would you please see if Cheryl has any bottled water? And let her know he may need a medivac."

If they couldn't get EMS in for LeBlack, they surely won't be able to get them in for him, either. Unless something is very different outside now…

Art rose and wove his way through clots of people standing in the aisleway. PC turned her attention back to Smitherson.

"Who is Fabella? Is she in trouble? Can we help her?"

"No." His voice wasn't much more than a whisper. "Not unless you have a time machine."

"Why's that?"

"They haven't made parts for her in decades. Now she's ruined."

PC remembered the photo Felicity had sent her. "Is Fabella a car? A red car?"

Smitherson's swallow looked painful, and PC winced on his behalf. "Yes. How did you know?"

"I saw a picture. I think it was a newspaper clipping."

He nodded. "Yes. Yes, we were in the paper." He sat up and yawed toward PC.

The detective caught him as he swayed into her. "Why were you in the paper?"

Smitherson sighed. "When my dad was courting my mom, he had a cherry red 1969 Coupe de Ville with a white vinyl roof." He breathed heavily.

"You okay?"

He nodded, then grimaced. "Yeah. My dad, he worked an extra job so he could buy that Cadillac. I think he loved it almost as much as he loved my mom. She said she felt like a queen when he picked her up in that car, because everyone turned their head to watch them go past. She couldn't help but marry a man with such an amazing car."

PC steadied him as he swayed.

"Anyway, my sister came along, and two doors was hard with the huge car seat for the baby. He covered the de Ville and parked it in his parents' barn after he bought a family-friendly car. Years after he died, my grandmother decided to sell the farm and move to town. We found the old de Ville, and I had it fixed up. Mom got so excited, riding in that car. Newspaper thought it was a great human-interest story."

"I can see why Fabella was important to you."

"And then he hit her. And like I said, there aren't parts… there aren't parts to fix her."

"Who hit Fabella?"

Smitherson's lips pulled back, almost in a snarl.

"LeBlack. LeBlack killed Fabella."

Chapter 12

PC's MOUTH FELL open. "Mack LeBlack hit Fabella? When?"

Smitherson sniffled. "This morning. Turning into the parking garage. He made a left turn on a red light and plowed right into us, Fabella and me. Then he got out of his truck and threatened me. Blamed the accident on me. Told me I'd better not report it as his fault, because his attorneys would sue me for everything I had. Let him try—he's not stealing anything from me, not today, not ever."

"Wow." PC was at a loss for words.

Art returned with a bottle of water and handed it to Smitherson, who took it gratefully.

The detective gathered her thoughts while he sipped, remembering the broken plastic in the driveway. "What happened then?"

Smitherson held the water in his mouth before he swallowed. "He drove into the garage and left me there. I used my phone app to file my claim and call a wrecker." His eyes closed for a moment. "But there was a group of people waiting for the shuttle and saw the whole thing. Three of them came up to me later and gave me their contact information, if I needed a witness."

"Really? Which ones?" Art sprung the question out of the blue.

"What?" Smitherson asked, his head rotating toward PC's self-appointed assistant.

"Which people said they would testify for you?" Art clarified.

Holding his goose egg, Smitherson swiveled his head, scanning the room. "Him." He pointed to Brady Michaels. "Him." A muscular man with wild, curly blond hair read a magazine in the back row. "And…. Her." She looked barely old enough for jury duty, in her houndstooth check skinny pants and cold shoulder black top.

"I am so sorry that happened to you, Mr. Smitherson. I'm a little concerned about your health—I think you have a concussion. Would you come with me—us—so Miss Cheryl can keep an eye on you?"

"Sure, I guess."

The three of them stood up, but Smitherson swayed a little. "Give me a sec for the room to stop spinning."

The trio made their way carefully to the front desk. Art moved one of the chairs against the wall for Smitherson to sit in while PC explained to Cheryl what had happened. She agreed to monitor him.

"Now what?" Art asked.

PC rubbed her forehead. She would prefer Art do something else, but she felt sorry for him. Even though he was older than her, he had a little brother vibe that made her think of Rocky. "Well, I suppose we could talk to Brady, and see if he can confirm the car wreck."

Art gave her a wan smile.

She sincerely hoped she wasn't being played. Once in a while, Rocky got one over on her. The other times, he regretted trying.

Brady stared at his phone in the back of the room. He didn't even look up when PC and Art sad down on either side. "What's up, Detective?"

"I understand you witnessed a car accident this morning."

Art nodded along for emphasis.

"It wasn't an accident. LeBlack deliberately rammed Peter. He's got push bars on the front of his ridiculous truck. He didn't get a scratch. I felt terrible for Peter, though. He'd clearly spent a lot of time and money restoring that car. It's probably totaled."

PC ran her tongue along the backs of her teeth. "You didn't think this was worth mentioning earlier?"

"You asked about *my* interactions with LeBlack, not whether I'd watched him terrorize other people."

PC's jaw clenched and released. "Do you think Mr. Smitherson harmed Mr. LeBlack?"

"Why would I think that?"

"It seems like you're trying to protect him."

Art chimed in. "Does he *need* protecting?"

Brady shifted in his seat. "I don't know. But I *do* know that he and I could happily share a chorus of *Ding, Dong the Witch is Dead*."

You're not the only ones. "Thanks for confirming the accident."

"Anytime. Not like I'm going anywhere."

PC and Art rose and walked down the aisle until they were safely out of earshot.

Art licked his lips as he nodded toward the young female witness. "Maybe we should get a second opinion from her?"

The detective raised an eyebrow. "She looks terrified. The last thing she needs is you leering at her."

"I wasn't leering."

PC's other eyebrow arched up.

"It wasn't leering. It was appreciating."

"I'm sure she doesn't need any appreciation right now, either."

Art's lips tightened, then he muttered something under his breath.

PC scanned the room. Purple Skirt Alice stood at the front, with a small group of people who seemed to be sporadically talking. She continued looking. French Braid Alice was in an animated discussion near the back.

Purple Skirt Alice was closer and would probably be easier to peel off from the group. The detective nodded in her direction. She led and Art followed. They stationed themselves close enough to eavesdrop on the knot of people that included Purple Skirt Alice.

A woman in a pink top shook her head. "No. Organic only means no synthetic fertilizers and pesticides. It doesn't have anything to do with that."

Purple Skirt Alice crossed her arms. "I'm sorry, if a tomato has fish DNA, there's no way it's organic." Her waist-length braid swung behind her like a metronome as her head moved back and forth.

The sole male in the group replied, "GMO and organic are two different things. They shouldn't be, but they are. Heirloom tomatoes aren't genetically engineered. Unless you count selective breeding."

"Fish genes in tomatoes! That isn't right. Is that so they can swim away if it floods?" Purple Skirt Alice gestured with one arm, the other still across her chest.

PC moved closer. "I apologize for butting in, but did you say there are fish genes in tomatoes? How does that even happen?"

"Gene splicing," Purple Skirt Alice growled.

"It's supposed to make the plants more frost tolerant. They used an Arctic fish, not sure what kind," the man in the group replied.

"Huh. Mama always said grocery store tomatoes don't taste anything like homegrown. But I've never noticed them tasting fishy." PC played up the part of the rube.

Art tried to join in the conversation. "That does sound kind of gross."

"You bet it's gross," Purple Skirt Alice said.

A woman who looked like an autumn lawn after a windy day in her red, orange, and yellow mottled top over khaki slacks *tsk tsked*. "Willow, calm down. If we want to produce enough food for the world's population, we have to make it more efficient, and crops have to be able to withstand wider temperature ranges."

Purple Skirt Alice whirled on her. "I am not uncalm. I also don't wish to be forced into the job of lab rat every time I eat."

Okay. So Purple Skirt Alice is actually called Willow.

"You know," Art said, "Mack LeBlack talked about this on his show a couple of weeks ago. Anybody catch that episode?"

The four people looked at each other, shaking their heads.

"Never heard of him," Willow said, her voice crisp. She turned back to her companions, jerking a thumb over her shoulder. "That guy back there? The one that dropped dead from a heart attack? Heart disease is the number one killer in the US. And you know when that became a thing? After the introduction of synthetic pesticides and frankenfoods. These things are killing us."

"Correlation doesn't prove causation," snapped the woman in orange.

It was the man's turn to cross his arms. "I think that has more to do with OSHA and vaccines. Well, that and a more sedentary workforce."

PC had enough of this discussion. It wasn't helping to find the second Alice. She started to ease away from the group. No one appeared to notice her and Art slip away.

He frowned. "Four down, one to go. What if the last one isn't named Alice?"

"I don't know. I guess we go around calling out the name 'Alice' and see if anyone turns around."

It better not come to that. That's a recipe for all kinds of awkward.

She looked toward the back of the room, where she'd last seen French Braid Alice.

The detective noticed that Toby was smiling. *He must have gotten a good update.* She turned to Art. "Can you give me a minute?"

"Sure."

PC made her way to the line of chairs.

Toby grinned when he saw her, but waited for her to get close before speaking. "DPS just arrived with the MRAPs and the Guard will be here in half an hour. Won't be much longer now."

"Good."

Or was it? Could a murderer be escaping when the door opened?

PC's phone vibrated. Felicity. "Excuse me. I have to take this." The detective tapped the SMS icon and read the message.

"I only found one Dallas Papadopoulos. Be careful. He served time for stalking."

Chapter 13

STALKING. OF COURSE *he did.* PC replied to Felicity's text. "Who did he stalk?"

The detective's eyes found Art's, and she waved him over.

"Any news?" he asked when he got near.

"This should be over soon."

"Yeah? What's changed?"

PC sat down. The day wasn't even half over, but she felt like it was going on eighteen hours. Stress had a way of concentrating time. "The cavalry just turned up."

He glanced at the door. "Good to know."

"There's one potential Alice left. I should go talk to her." She was already searching the room for French Braid Alice.

Art forced a breath loudly out through his nose, but he made no other protest.

PC spotted the braid and the black dress with its ghostly damask pattern and picked her way through the ever-moving groups of people. French Braid Alice had finished her animated discussion and was scribbling on a scrap of paper.

The detective coughed. "You going to sell your story to the news?"

French Braid Alice looked up with a furrowed brow. "What?"

PC gestured to the scrawl-covered paper. "You writing down the details to keep them fresh in your mind?"

"Sort of. Dr. Bennet and I were discussing Meursault's relationship with his mother as the basis for his dissociative behavior."

Who? The detective looked around the room.

"Well, if he wasn't a fictional character from the 40s, I suppose we could ask him. *The Stranger*? Albert Camus?"

A dusty memory from college literature class tumbled from the deeper recesses of her brain and landed in her frontal lobe with a dry cough. "That guy. Hadn't thought about him in years. That's extremely rare. I mean, it's true that most violent crime is spontaneous, but it's also opportunistic. Not random. It could happen, that a man is walking down the beach and shoots a random stranger for no reason. But there's almost always a reason. Unless you're going to pin it on Poe's Imp of the Perverse."

French Braid Alice broke into a grin. "One of Poe's lesser-known works. You are well-read."

Any chance you're related to him? "Well, I wrote a research paper on Edgar Allan Poe. So perhaps I'm well-read on a specific author."

"I resemble that remark. I'm Dr. Newsome. But you can call me Cynthia. I took a class in post-World War II European literature. Loved it, but it kicked my butt. By the end of it, I was wondering how much of Theatre of the Absurd was theater and how much just absurd."

PC replied with the only Jean Paul Sartre quote she knew. "Hell is other people."

"Most people misinterpret what he meant, but sometimes, I wholeheartedly agree. Hopefully, there will be an exit, and soon." She tapped her pen on the edge of the chair.

"It's nice to meet you, Cynthia. I go by PC. I'm pretty certain—"

"Your parents named you 'Pretty Certain?' Really?"

PC chuckled. "No. They named me Primrose Corvina, and I'm very sure we'll be out of here soon."

"Corvina? Was one of your parents fond of ravens?"

The detective rubbed her arm. "I don't know about that, but it was my grandmother's name."

"Of course."

"I won't keep you. You're clearly ready to get back to your writing."

It was Cynthia's turn to laugh. "Is it that obvious? I'm sorry. It was very refreshing to meet someone with an appreciation for literature, though."

PC smiled, nodded, and strolled away.

Her phone vibrated. Felicity with more information. "Savannah Turner's shop is called 'Bramblemuffins.' Some things should not be crocheted. Just sayin."

Savannah, Savannah. What am I going to do with you? You are the most suspicious. And yet, of all the people who had a physical interaction with LeBlack, you are the only one with seemingly no motive. This is no Algerian beach for you to hunt a random victim. And if this is a murder, it took planning.

"TY, Felicity. I know it seems weird, but could you check and see if there are any negative reviews of her shop from either Mack LeBlack or Troy Lendon?"

Seems a stretch, but people have been killed for less.

PC sat down next to Art, shaking her head. "Not Alice."

Art pulled at a large, coarse hair embedded in the fabric of his pants. "Now what do we do?"

That is the biggest hair I've ever seen. What kind of pet do you have, Art? PC thought.

"Well, we seem to be out of Alices. We know that Elvira Ravenstone is really Alice Lewis. But what about Alice Poe? None of the women who matched Savannah's vague description were her. At least I don't think so, but I suppose it's possible that one of them is also using an alias."

Art looked toward the front of the room where Savannah sat crocheting at a high rate of speed. "What if she made Alice up, unaware that there were two real Alices in the room? It's not the most common name."

"That's a possibility. But it's odd that while the shawl, ring, and scarf all point to her, she's the only one who doesn't seem to have a motive. Means and opportunity, yes, but not motive."

"Not that you know of, anyway. Everyone has secrets." Art dropped the hair on the floor, where it lay rigidly between them, a dark, matte crack across the slate-colored carpet.

PC nodded. "True." Then she leaned over and picked up the hair. "Okay. I have to ask. Do you have a pet werewolf or something?"

Art snorted with laughter. "No. I told you I work at the zoo. I'm a large mammal keeper. Right now, I'm working with rhinos, but I also fill in with the elephants as needed. You know, like if someone's out sick or on vacation."

"That explains it. Must be an interesting job. Do you travel much?"

"Not really—conferences and picking up or dropping off new animals. Also, as part of the endangered species work we do, we trade individual specimens to promote genetic diversity. And sometimes, just because you have a boy and a girl, it doesn't mean they're a match."

"Huh. Never really thought about rhinoceri needing a love connection."

"Actually, more than one rhinoceros is also rhinoceros. Like deer or fish. And a group is called a crash—bet you didn't know that."

"What else would they be called?" *What else, indeed?*

"One of our girls, Seraphina, had routine dental work last week. Rhinos, if you don't know, can make a high-pitched, noise—sounds like a mixture of kittens and dolphins."

He chuckled. "You have to hear it. Anyway, while she was recovering from anesthesia, she kept trilling, then randomly barking. There's an African grey parrot down the hall who just lives in the clinic, because he's only got one wing. He heard Seraphina and started imitating her. Now any time the rhino keepers come into the clinic, he starts up with rhino noises. And not just the two of us that were there that day. Any rhino keeper. Those parrots are scary smart."

PC smacked her lips. "Kittens and dolphins? I'm having a tough time imagining that."

Art pulled out his phone and unlocked it. His lips pursed. "I would show you a video, if I had a signal." He put the device back into his pocket.

The detective gave a little shrug and a smile. "It's okay. I can look it up later. But back to Alice. I'll go around and see if I can find her."

"What am I supposed to do?"

"Keep an eye on Savannah. Either she's completely innocent, or she's an excellent performer."

The detective got up and surveyed the room. A covey of women huddled at the front of the room. May as well start there. She listened to their conversation for a moment.

"Oh, we saw some of those in Las Vegas! They were amazing."

"Have you seen that French lady? She doesn't use any curtains or tubes, or anything. Her clothes change instantly, in full view of the audience."

"How do they do that?"

"I spent hours watching DIY YouTube videos after we saw that show. They use Velcro, magnets, specially constructed clothing—skirts or shirts that roll up and tuck into a pouch the audience can't see. I don't know how anyone came up with all of that."

"Did you see Cirque de Soleil while you were there?"

"Always amazing. I didn't know the human body could do those things."

"It's almost like they don't have bones."

"They can fold up like a piece of paper and get into containers that you wouldn't think a human could get into, not without going through a blender first."

"Girl, my husband wishes I could bend like that. I told him when he looks like one of those guys, I'll take up contortion classes."

"Well, we saw the no-one-under-18 show. That was… something else. Don't take your mother."

The women laughed.

PC approached the group and laid her hand on her jaw. "Oh, my goodness! Alice? Is that you?"

No one responded to the name Alice, but a few of the women glanced at her as if making threat assessments. One lady whose back was to PC turned around.

PC's hand shifted from her jaw to her mouth, then she pulled it away. "I am so sorry. I was sure you were my former neighbor, Alice. My mistake."

The detective scurred away before anyone could comment. Her phone vibrated. *What do you have for me, Felicity?*

It was Rose. "Will you be back in time for lunch?"

"Probably not." She had no way of knowing when her mother actually sent the text or whether she'd watched the news. PC really hoped her mother kept to her usual habit of watching TV reruns during the day. She smiled to herself as she remembered Rose never missed an episode of *Night Court* back in the day. High school, and then college activities kept PC busy, and she had rarely watched the show.

PC was choosing her next target when her device buzzed again. *That was quick! Could this be a sweet spot?* She pulled out her phone.

Not Rose, but Felicity. "Alice Lewis, as noted previously. Alice Poe and her son Carmichael sued LeBlack for spreading panic during Hurricane Charlie fifteen years ago. Dismissed. Did find LeBlack was arrested re: assaulting Peter Smitherson. Charges dropped."

Chapter 14

Now that was something she could research. Well, Toby could research for her. He'd have access to the database with all that lovely arrest record and case disposition information. Why did LeBlack assault Smitherson? Did he intimidate him into dropping the charges? Or was it something else?

PC hot-footed it over to the officer. "Hey, Toby? This may not mean anything, but I've heard that LeBlack was arrested for assault on Peter Smitherson."

"And?"

"I was wondering if you could verify."

"Why can't you do it yourself?"

The detective rubbed her temple. "Did I mention I was retired?"

"Are you trying to get me fired?"

PC held up her phone. "I'm not asking for confidential information. Court records are public. But I don't have internet."

Toby looked around. PC followed his eyes to Smitherson, squirming in his chair. "Him? Okay. Give me a minute."

The keyboard rattled under his fingers. She couldn't look at Smitherson. His gyrations only reminded her that she needed to pee. As she scanned the room, looking for a potential Alice Poe, she realized there were too many women to approach each one in the time frame she had. Prioritization. That was the key.

"Got it. It looks like what happened is that LeBlack approached Smitherson and his mother at a restaurant and wanted to buy Smitherson's classic car... Mrs. Smitherson declined... LeBlack verbally aggressive... restaurant manager called police... LeBlack taken into custody, but bailed out almost as soon as he got there... DA determined insufficient evidence and dropped charges... Complaint letter in the file from Smitherson that LeBlack's attorney was harassing him and threatening frivolous lawsuits to bankrupt him."

PC rubbed her chin. "I suppose that's why LeBlack rammed his car and threatened to sic his attorneys on Smitherson again. Also gives Smitherson an excellent reason to permanently solve his LeBlack problem."

"Where's your sidekick?"

The detective rolled her eyes, but made sure he wasn't standing behind her when she spoke. "He's surveilling a suspect." *Speaking of which...* "Would you look up one more thing for me?"

"What's that?"

"Is it true that Dallas Papadopoulos served time for stalking? And if so, who did he stalk?"

Toby's fingers danced over the keys.

PC scanned the room for her persons of interest.

Why hadn't Brady told her about the petition for his ouster?

Elvira didn't go into detail about the arson and injuries to her sister. *Too incriminating?*

Dallas failed to mention his stalking incarceration, but why would he?

Savannah's Etsy shop wasn't the same one the scarf came from, so no big deal.

Smitherson would probably be angry and embarrassed by the bullying he'd received at LeBlack's hands.

"I found him. Dallas Papadopoulos served a year and a half of a five-year sentence for aggravated stalking of Brenda Mason, the Channel 9 weather girl. He violated a restraining order she had against him when he tried to break into her house, carrying zip ties. She moved to the Atlanta station affiliate before he got out of jail."

"Don't blame her."

She turned her eyes back to Papadopoulos, calmly scrolling on his phone.

You're obsessed enough for an attempted kidnap, but are you obsessed enough to kill?

"Thanks for looking those up, Toby. Any updates on the situation outside?"

"Yeah. The rioters have been contained. They're being arrested, but there's a lot of 'em. It'll take some time. But the situation is under control."

"Glad to hear that. With any luck, they'll open the flood doors soon and take us out through the tunnels."

Toby shrugged. "I haven't heard anything about that."

If someone had killed LeBlack, she'd better figure it out soon so the culprit could be detained when the doors opened. She had a lot of suspects to choose from.

"Alright. Thanks again."

She headed toward Brady Michaels. He saw her coming and watched her move through the crowd and sit next to him.

"So, I heard a rumor, Doc. Did you say there is a petition being circulated to get you fired?"

His lips moved into a sardonic smile. "It's true. Widely known, in certain circles. It's also known that I've been trying to get LeBlack federally charged for violation of the Endangered Species Act over his turtle egg atrocity." He let out a deep breath. "I can't go into detail, but I'm suing LeBlack, the local station, and their network for defamation of character over the petition. It's a good thing he's got so many enemies, because I couldn't afford the lawyers otherwise. More than one looking to make a name for themselves by taking down LeBlack."

PC clicked her tongue. "You're not getting support from Parks and Wildlife?"

"Oh, my department's great. They're doing everything they can. It's the state Attorney General who's dragging his feet on the turtles. I'm on my own with the petition, though."

"Who started it?"

"One of LeBlack's employees. They're getting sued, too."

"Well, it looks like a big thorn has been pulled out of your side."

Brady snickered. "That it does. If only he'd brought as much happiness in life as he has in death. I'm sure once word gets out, there will be parties all over town. They may even organize a parade."

"That's grim."

"Everyone is free to choose. No one is free of the consequences of their choices." He interlaced his fingers over his stomach.

PC stood up. "Well. Good luck with your litigation."

"Thank you."

She'd better check on Art. Didn't want him getting antsy and talking to other suspects and getting them stirred up. He was still where she'd left him, so that was a good sign. She headed in his direction.

"Anything good?" he asked as she sat down.

"They're hauling the rioters off to jail. We should be out of here pretty soon."

He grinned. "Good." He cocked his head toward Savannah. "She hasn't done anything but crochet. I think she'll be finished with that blanket before we get out of here." Art scratched his jaw.

"Yeah. Unless she's secretly Alice Poe, I don't think she had anything to do with it."

Art's brow furrowed. "How do you know she isn't?"

"I don't. It is possible that Alice Poe is pretending to be Savannah Turner, hoping that her frame job is so obvious that she escapes in the guise of Savannah Turner while the cops are looking for Alice Poe."

"You think the frame is that badly done?" The would-be detective crossed his arms.

"Yes. The problem with that is that while Alice had the same means and opportunity as anyone else, and we've only looked at the five people I saw exchange something with LeBlack, she doesn't seem to have nearly as much motive. Although there could be someone else I didn't see. Seems like you can't sling a cat without hitting someone who hates Mack LeBlack."

Art raised his eyebrows. "I would recommend against slinging cats."

PC massaged the bridge of her nose. "I would never sling actual cats, Art." She pointed to the chair on the other side of her companion. "I left my notes over here. Would you mind handing them to me?"

She didn't care if he'd looked at them. Between her own personal shorthand and medical-quality handwriting, no one could make sense of them but her. She'd have to type them up for whomever was performing the actual investigation.

The detective stared at the door for a few moments. She was grateful that LeBlack and his possible murder would cease to be her problem soon. But in the meantime, she couldn't sit on her hands and make it easy for a killer to escape.

PC curled the pages into a roll. "I'm going to talk to Elvira some more."

"I can come with you."

"I'd prefer you didn't, Art. I know you're just trying to help, but I think she'd be more likely to speak with me rather than us."

He gestured in frustration. "Maybe I should just ask Savannah to teach me to crochet."

"Great idea. It would give you something to do."

He glowered.

Elvira sat alone at the back of the room, as far away from LeBlack's corpse as possible, sneaking a vape. PC took the chair next to her, shielding her from Toby, who probably had too much on his plate at the moment to police e-cigarettes. But then again, he could be great at multi-tasking.

"Why didn't you want to tell me about the fire?"

"You don't beat around the bush."

"No. Saves time."

The psychic twirled a lock of blue and green hair around her index finger. "It's too hard. Insurance mostly took care of the shop. But Sabrina…" Elvira hung her head. When she spoke again, her voice was barely above a whisper. "My sister was so beautiful. She did some modeling locally and was saving money to go to New York. Not anymore. There's only so much medical science can do to treat severe burns. She's tried to kill herself three times since the fire. We tried taking LeBlack to court, but the judge said that just because one of his crazy followers set my business on fire doesn't mean LeBlack is responsible. Case dismissed."

"I'm really sorry."

"She was working for me part-time to make ends meet. In some ways, I feel like it was my fault this happened to her. Not that I'd wish it on anyone else. I'd trade places with her if I could." Elvira sniffled.

"This shouldn't have happened to anyone."

"Yeah? And you know what's even worse? The guy who set the fire is out of jail in three months. I'm worried he's going to come after us again."

"You can ask for a restraining order."

"Is it printed on bulletproof paper?"

It was PC's turn to study the floor. She unrolled her notes and fanned herself. The room was suddenly stuffy. "I wish it was."

"Are you some kind of spy?"

"What?" PC jerked her head around and hit herself in the nose with the fan.

Elvira nodded toward PC's makeshift air conditioner. "Is that some kind of spy alphabet?"

"No just my notes."

"Don't take this the wrong way, but you should consider a transfer-resistant foundation."

PC scrunched her face.

Elvira pointed to a tan smudge on the top page. "Makeup."

"So it is." PC got to her feet. *I don't even wear foundation.* "I'm really sorry to hear about your sister. And the arsonist being released."

The psychic took a hit on her e-cig. "Thanks."

If someone did that to Daisy, I'd certainly have some ideas about their swift demise.

The detective moved to the aisleway where Toby sat with LeBlack. Out of the corner of her eye, she saw Art rising and moving in her direction. She sighed inwardly. There might be a full minute to talk to Toby before Art arrived.

"Hey, Toby. Any updates?"

His mouth fell into an easy smile. "They're almost done out there. It should be any time now."

"Good." PC licked her lips. "Do you know if a crime scene unit will be waiting to come in when the doors open?"

Toby's shoulder twitched. "Don't know. They know there's a decedent."

"Well, I have some information to share with them. Never did find Alice Poe. I'm probably just about out of time, though."

"So, what's the scoop?" Art stood close to the chairs that cordoned off LeBlack's body.

"We're almost out of here," Toby replied.

"That's great!" Art's voice was loud enough that a few people turned around. He lowered the volume. "I wonder if they'll have the car parts in the parking garage entrance cleaned up by the time we get out."

Toby's jaw clenched. "Probably not. It's been kinda busy out there."

Art's lips thinned into a school-marmish expression. "That car fender'll block traffic. And anybody could get a flat from the smaller pieces of metal and glass laying around."

"I think it was a bumper, not a fender in the driveway," PC said.

Toby's excited expression turned sour. "Why don't you take a taxi home and come pick up your car tomorrow?"

"Are you kidding? I can't get out of here fast enough. Everyone's been acting like it's some big cocktail party." Art turned toward the body. "But that's one heck of an elephant in the room."

And then it clicked.

PC locked eyes with Toby. "I know who Alice is."

Chapter 15

PC TURNED TO her left. "I know how you did it, Art. Or should I say, Carmichael?"

His mouth dropped open. "What? I can't believe what I'm hearing."

"Your mother—Alice Poe—got the jury summons, not you. But she's bedridden—no way she'd be able to serve. When you heard Mack LeBlack complaining about jury duty, you seized the opportunity. You bought that blindingly pink shawl to draw focus away from your face. People would remember that atrocity, but not necessarily the face behind it. Once you used your poisoner's ring to get carfentanil into LeBlack's bloodstream, you ditched the shawl, the scarf, and the ring."

"Carfentanil? What's that?" Art's eyebrows crinkled.

PC sighed. "Don't play dumb. You know what it is. It was developed especially to sedate large animals, like elephants. And then you told me you were a large mammal keeper at the zoo, I should have known then. But it took you saying 'car fender'll' and 'elephant' so close to each other that the pieces fell into place."

"Coincidences happen. You can't prove those two things are related."

"When the lights went out, it must have felt like serendipity. It gave you the opportunity to plant the scarf, glove, and ring in Savannah's purse."

Art grinned and shook his head. "This is all conjecture."

"Is it? You told me that your mother was catatonic. But you had me stumped for a while. I kept looking at the women I thought might be Alice, but none of them were old enough. I tried to work out ways that they could have gotten make up or a mask off, but I just couldn't get there. But it was you wearing the makeup, not them." She flicked a fingernail across his jaw and it came up with foundation.

He took a step backward. "It's socially acceptable these days for men to wear makeup."

Toby cocked an eyebrow.

PC continued. "That may be. You appear to be in your mid-sixties—older than me. However, you told me you used to watch Night Court with your mom when you were a kid. My mother also watched that show, but it came on the last year I was in high school. You're younger than me. By a lot. The time difference didn't hit me until Elvira pointed out the makeup on the paper."

"I'm not sure what you're talking about."

"Earlier, when I'd asked you to hand me my notes, you scratched your jaw first. Then Elvira pointed out that there was a smear of makeup on the paper. I don't wear foundation, so it had to have been from your hands."

Art smirked. "Wasn't Alice described as wearing a dress, with flowers on it?"

"She was."

"I'm wearing pants and a plain white shirt."

Toby looked at PC. "How do you get around that?"

The detective took a step forward, reached under Art's hoodie, and yanked on the shoulder. A flap of black fabric, decorated with large watercolor roses and leaves, dangled across his chest.

Art's eyes blazed and his hands grabbed at the cloth.

PC gestured toward the shirt. "I hadn't been able to figure that out, either. Then I heard some ladies talking about quick change acts in Las Vegas and I remembered that Art went there to pick up an elephant. When I'd sent him to get some paper, he came back with a paperclip stuck on his shoulder. I realized then that there must be magnets holding his shirt together."

"That's preposterous!" growled Art as he took a step away from them.

"Not at all." PC nodded to Toby. "Let me tell you what I think happened. Art's parents were on that ill-fated bus that got rear-ended and caught fire during the Hurricane Charlie evacuation. His father was killed. His mother survived, but she had a lot of trauma, physical and mental. Art—I mean Carmichael—blamed LeBlack for stampeding the evacuees and causing the traffic nightmare, but the lawsuit went nowhere. He monitored LeBlack by listening to his show on the radio, hoping for a chance at revenge."

The former assistant investigator seethed.

PC continued. "When LeBlack began publicly complaining about jury duty, it was a lucky break that Carmichael's mother got a summons for that same day. But he had to plan carefully. And he came up with a pretty good plan. Even swiped his alias from Sir Arthur Conan Doyle and tried to be Dr. Watson to my Sherlock Holmes.

Toby snorted.

The detective nodded. "He came dressed as Alice Poe, bringing the eye-breaking shawl to plant on some unsuspecting older woman once he had done the deed."

Carmichael took another step back. "You can't prove anything."

"I believe I can prove everything. But I'm getting to that. He used the blue nitrile glove to protect his hand when he put the ring on and took it off, as the sharp edge of the setting had been treated with carfentanil, which he helped himself to when he was in the vet clinic with the rhino getting dental work. Dressed as Alice, he patted LeBlack's hand. The drug would have absorbed through the skin, but he wanted to make sure by getting it into LeBlack's bloodstream."

"Pretty smart," Toby said.

"He then quickly pawned the hideous shawl off on Savannah Turner. When LeBlack began to react to the drug and all eyes were on him, Carmichael stood at the front of the room and converted his floral skirt to a white shirt with the help of magnets along the shoulder and side seams. And that's why he wore the hoodie, to cover up the lumpy joins and bulge where the extra skirt fabric is hidden. It only took a few seconds, and he was already wearing the pants underneath. He just needed to get rid of the shawl, glove, and ring. The power going out provided the perfect opportunity for him to further set up Savannah."

Carmichael sighed loudly. "You still cannot prove any of this."

"That's where you're wrong. Forensics will be able to get your DNA out of the blue glove and probably the scarf and shawl."

"And what are they going to compare it to? I've never been arrested." He gave her a wicked smile.

"You remember that gum you were chewing? The one you spat out into the paper?"

Carmichael's eyes widened.

PC smiled. "Officer Jensen here witnessed you spitting it out, and it's probably on camera as well. They can test that known DNA sample to what they find in the glove to get their match."

"I don't consent!"

Toby chuckled. "Too bad. You threw it away. You have no rights to it anymore. Finders keepers."

Carmichael lunged for the paper envelopes resting on the chair cordon. Toby grabbed him and wrestled him to the ground. People gasped and turned to watch the drama. PC removed the handcuffs from Toby's belt and the officer snapped them on Carmichael's writhing wrists.

Light spilled in as the door cracked open, revealing SWAT officers in full tactical gear. People cheered and shouted. The officers waved them toward the door.

PC sat with Toby and the prone Carmichael "Well, I guess they'll want a full report."

Chapter 16

PC PULLED INTO Rose's driveway. *Home again, home again, jiggety jog.* Her father had always said that when they pulled into the driveway after a trip. Traces of him lingered everywhere.

Being in a room packed with people all day left her drained and depleted. Crowds bothered her less when she was younger. The detective had stopped by the hospital to visit her friends, but they'd already been released. She'd check on the critters, say hello to Mama, and have a little nap.

Inside the house, Cordite started barking as soon as she got out of the car. His excitement made her smile. Dogs didn't do ulterior motives.

She trudged inside. The pup wagged his entire body, and she scooped him up in her arms. Rose and Terry sat in the living room on the couch. He was working a crossword puzzle, and she was reading a book. They did look cute together.

Rose looked up. "You didn't get picked, honey?"

"No." What her mother didn't know wouldn't hurt her—knowing about all the nastiness in the jury pool would only upset her, anyway.

Terry grinned back at her. "Probably less stressful that way. But a long way to drive for a cup of coffee."

Less stressful? Don't I wish. "Yeah. But I did get to talk to some interesting people, so there's that."

PC continued into the kitchen, then out the back door. She set Cordite down so he could water the tree, then walked to the back fence to check on the animals. Guinevere and Arthur stood together under the barn awning, snoozing in the shade. Hazel grazed lazily underneath a tree. The chickens stopped their pecking and scratching, on alert for a bonus serving of hen scratch. When it wasn't forthcoming, they returned to their bug hunt.

Tiredness had seeped all the way into PC's bones. It was still a little early for donkey rations, but since she was out here, she may as well get them fed. Just in case.

When she had finished, Cordite trotted up to her, panting.

"You're right, Cordie. It's way too hot out here. Bet it's over a hundred."

They went back into the house, where the little dog flopped on the cool wood floor while PC got herself some water. She lay down on her bed and fell into oblivion.

The detective drifted up from the abyss of sleep, a persistent noise in her right ear. Her eyeballs had stuck to her eyelids, and she had to move them back and forth to spread the little moisture there was around enough to open her eyes. She finally identified the sound as her phone. Her 7 AM alarm, in fact. *Wow. How did I get too old for a murder investigation so soon?*

She and Cordite got up and took care of the outside critters. When PC brought the eggs in, she debated about whether to cook her own breakfast or treat herself to the City Café. After fifteen hours of sleep, she was starved. Rocky had made a pot of coffee before he'd left for work, so she had some of that.

Rose sat at the dining table, still in her nightgown and bathrobe, reading the Possumwood Press and eating buttered toast.

"Hey, Mama? You interested in going to the City Café?"

"That's sweet of you to ask, honey. But Terry and I are goin' to Horice to the Mallard Museum, then we're gonna have lunch there. You go on ahead, though."

"Have fun." PC rinsed her cup and put it in the dishwasher. She thought about making her own breakfast after all, but considered the clean-up. She grabbed her car keys.

A half-empty cup of coffee sat near her plate, and the residue of poached eggs and hash browns left a bright yellow smear across the white china. PC read through her email on her phone.

The noise of a chair scraping across the floor made her look up.

"Mornin' Donovan." The police chief settled his tall frame at her table.

"Hey, Woody." *What does he want?*

"Well, what do you know? We've made it through half of August without a murder. Maybe your streak is broken."

This is what you invaded my space to tell me? "Maybe."

"Are you planning on being around next month?"

"Why?"

"I need an extra volunteer to run our dunk tank at the county fair. We're raising money to buy a modern radio system for the department. There's an unacceptable number of dead spots with the old equipment. It wasn't new when I started here twenty years ago. I have one shift I can't cover, and I was wondering if you'd be available to help us out?"

There was a long list of things that PC would rather do than run a dunk tank. But then again, she might get a chance to throw a few balls while Woody was in the hot seat.

"When is it?"

"Second weekend in September."

Knowing full well she had no plans, she made a show of checking the calendar on her phone. "I might have a slot. What time?"

"First shift on Saturday morning—8 AM."

"Until when?"

"10:30. Shouldn't be too busy then."

Odds were, she'd be there anyway, but probably not that early. But it was for a good cause. Possumwood's police radios were antique, and she'd prefer the added safety of reliable communication for her friends at PPD.

"Sure. Sign me up."

"Okay. Make sure you bring dry clothes."

"Wait. What?"

Woody chuckled. "Kidding. I just need you to take tickets and pass out softballs."

"I can handle that."

"Appreciate you helping out." He sipped his coffee.

Is there anything else you want? PC blotted her lips with a paper napkin.

He'd made himself comfortable and it might not be easy to dislodge him.

The chief set the mug down and leaned toward PC. "I bought a Harley."

"A motorcycle?"

"Yeah. I've always wanted one. I thought I'd get it before... I got too old to enjoy it."

"Good. Now you can infiltrate the Possumwood chapter of the Banditos."

Woody snorted.

PC couldn't help but smile at him. "But don't worry. You're only a year older than me—you've got a long time before you're old."

"Maybe. But life can change in an instant. You of all people should know that."

"Is it red?"

"Red?"

"Well, the typical mid-life crisis toy is a red sports car, but I guess a motorcycle works, too."

"Are you saying I've got the middle-age crazies?"

"Does the shoe fit?"

"No. But I can see why it happens. What are you waiting to do, Donovan?" His eyes were somber.

"You okay, Woody?"

"Why wouldn't I be? I got me a brand-new hog." He got up, leaving his coffee cup on PC's table.

She watched him amble out the door.

Good for you, Woody. Good for you.

PC had lost interest in her email. She finished her coffee, got out her keys, and went to pay her check.

A few minutes later, the bells on the door jangled as PC entered *The Best Little Art Gallery in Texas*.

The proprietor grinned at her. "PC! This is a pleasant surprise."

"So… Drew. I was just wondering. Do you have any more of those entry forms for the art show at the fair?"

If you enjoyed this book, please consider leaving a review at your favorite book site. Reviews help other readers find and enjoy new books!

Other books by Holly Dey:

Manor of Death: The Possumwood Mysteries Book 1

Death on the Half Shell: The Possumwood Mysteries Book 2

Azalea Trail of Death: The Possumwood Mysteries Book 3

Death Re-Enacted: The Possumwood Mysteries Book 4

Death Rides a Bobcat: The Possumwood Mysteries Book 5

Key to Death: The Possumwood Mysteries Book 6

Death Curated: The Possumwood Mysteries Book 7

Pool of Death: The Possumwood Mysteries Book 8

All Death No Cattle: The Possumwood Mysteries Book 9

Death is Lager than Life: The Possumwood Mysteries Book 10

Art of Death: The Possumwood Mysteries Book 11

Little Town of Death-Lehem: The Possumwood Mysteries Book 12

Winter: Boxset Collection Books 1-3

Spring: Boxset Collection Books 4-6

Summer: Boxset Collection Books 7-9

Fall: Boxset Collection Books 10-12

All of the Possumwood Mysteries are available in

Large Print Editions